The Comanche Girl's Prayer

Angela Castillo

ISBN: 1517450284
ISBN-13: 978-1517450281

To the teachers.

Author's Note

History is filled with tragic stories, but the fate of many Native American groups must be one of the most sorrowful occurrences in the history of our United States. Few groups were as notorious as the Comanche. But the people of this fierce, courageous nation were brought to their knees by starvation and forced to acclimate at a reservation in Fort Sill, Oklahoma.

This book is a 'what-if.' What if a small group of people broke away from a reservation and camped out in the Texas wilderness, in order to be free? Accounts exist of families secretly living on the lands of ranchers and farmers, working for and trading with the owners.

It is a stretch of the imagination to accept this could happen, but not impossible. I have written this book with every attempt to make it as historically accurate as possible, and have found enough material to write dozens of books.

I also want to mention that I've made every attempt to be respectful of the Native American culture. Every word has been written in the hopes to educate and edify, with all due respect.

Acknowledgments

Thank you to Cherie Haines, Gloria Haines and April Haines. You are the best sisters anyone could ever have.

Thank you to all my friends at Scribophile, who helped me, once again, labor through a book.

Thank you to Cherie for a great photo, Sara Vanderbush for being 'Soonie' on my cover, and Elaina Lee with "For the Muse Design" for a lovely cover design.

And thank you to Robyn Carter, Britany Dooley, and Rebecca Walz. Your friendships have carried me through the years in ways you will never know.

1
A New Path

Dozens of locusts thrummed from the treetops. The mournful melody filled Soonie's ears in unshakable cadence.

Powerful as the sound became, Soonie's own heart, pounding against her faded calico dress, seemed louder. Her leg cramped, but she didn't dare to move. Squeezing her eyes shut, she fought to ignore the pain.

As a child, Soonie had played hundreds of games of hide-n-seek and had always been the last one found. *But never when the lives of my companions were at stake.*

Tersa and Bright Flower hunched beside her. Rocks towered around them, bushes sprouting from cracks like little girls carrying bouquets. The two men crouched a few feet ahead, drab clothing melting in with the trees and dappled sunlight.

Soonie swallowed a cough. Her canteen hung from her belt, but she couldn't reach for it. The slightest movement might cause the brush to sway, or create a gravel slide to alert the approaching travelers. She and her companions could not be seen.

She wasn't quite sure how Uncle Isak had caught wind of the travelers coming down the road. Perhaps he noticed a hawk's unusual flight pattern in the sky over the hills. Or maybe he heard a warning note in the squirrels' chatter. He had a sense for these things, instincts that had saved his own life and many other souls more than once.

This was the third time they had been forced off the road to hide from travelers. The further north they journeyed, the more the risk grew. Folks in this area watched for renegades. If caught, a Comanche of full blood could be beaten, imprisoned, or even lynched.

Uncle Isak glanced back at her, eyes shaded by the brim of his hat. Like her other companions, he wore clothing associated with town folks. He smiled reassuringly, small wrinkles forming around his eyes.

Unable to stand it any longer, she reached down to rub her aching calf. *Lord, we put our safety in your hands.*

Doves burst from a thicket and darted to higher trees over the path, and sun-dried dirt crunched under hooves.

They're coming.

Soonie pretended she was part of the earth, imagined herself melting into it like water, smoothing into the cracks, disappearing from sight.

Two men on horseback and two in a buckboard wagon paraded through the pass. At first they appeared tiny as tin soldiers, but soon were close enough that Soonie could hit one of them with a well-aimed stone.

One burly fellow removed his hat and ran a hand through hair so white it gleamed in the sunlight. "How much longer you reckon till we get to the ridge?"

Soonie could barely hear the younger man's reply through the locusts' song. "Don't know, Pa. Mebbie a day."

The conversation continued, with loud laughter, and ribald jokes that warmed Soonie's cheeks. On occasion, one of the men would stare up into the rocks, and the six on the hill tensed, hands on weapons.

But what will we do, if the call is made and the hill is charged? Soonie touched the hilt of her own knife, a gift from her brother, Wylder. The idea was flight, always flight. *Could I strike out to defend myself? The others?*

The men disappeared down the road, and everyone hiding relaxed. A very long time passed before Uncle Isak nodded. Soonie and the rest of the group followed him back to the clearing where they had left the horses.

The party continued on for several hours. Saddles had become a sort of home. Soonie, being accustomed to her horse's gaits and habits, would be fine for a few hours. But as the day grew warmer, sweat would start a slow trickle down her back and front, until she was drenched.

Women's' underthings were not meant for days of riding, especially the cotton petticoats Soonie had brought from home. On the second day of the journey, Tersa offered her a pair of deerskin leggings, and they had been a salvation. Her legs were grateful for the soft fabric protecting them from the worst of the saddle's chafing. They stayed hidden under her full skirt, along with her moccasins. Her feet would have been blistered and pinched in leather button-up shoes.

The August heat arrived early. The group started before dawn, took breaks during the hottest hours, and traveled into the night.

Soonie's horse, Stone Brother, snorted. The Indian pony had carried her through many an adventure, but was not accustomed to trips of this length.

"I know, dear." She patted his white and gold splotched neck. "We'll stop soon."

Tersa and Bright Flower were both a few years older than nineteen-year-old Soonie. Their horses' reins stayed tied to the saddle horns while they rode, keeping their hands free. Soonie could speak fluent Comanche, but she wasn't close enough to hear the words. From the gestures, she guessed the discussion was about cooking. Thick, dark hair blew above their shoulders, cut short in the Comanche style.

Uncle Isak and the other man, Wind Catcher, rode in silence. Both wore wide-brimmed hats to hide long, thick braids rolled neatly beneath them.

In the small town of Bastrop, Texas, where Soonie was from, one or two Comanche people would have evoked curiosity and perhaps a few questions. Most of the folks in town accepted the Comanche blood running through her veins. Bastrop gathered people like a magpie collected shiny trinkets, and those of assorted heritages and cultures strolled through the town streets.

A copse of cypress trees stretched long, feathered branches over a hollow, like a giant bird protecting its nest. The trees sent out thick, greedy roots to a meandering stream. *The perfect place for camp.*

As though Uncle Isak could hear her thoughts, he held up his hand. They all stopped.

The earth welcomed her feet. *Solid ground and soft grass to boot.* The scent of cool, moist earth mixed with a whiff of pollen from sun-warmed Indian Blanket flowers nodding by the water.

Soonie led Stone Brother to the stream for a drink as she rubbed him down with a handful of dried leaves. While he sucked up the water, her sore ankles pled their case. She dropped to the bank and tore off her moccasins.

Zillia would be scandalized if she knew I had my ankles bare, where these men could see them. On second thought, her best friend would probably have shared her weariness and dunked in her own toes.

A wry smile tugged at the corner of Soonie's lips. Zillia was done with adventures for a while, at least the kinds involving long journeys. Moments before the group set off, she had pulled Soonie aside to share a secret.

"Wylder and I will have a little one soon. February, I think," she had whispered excitedly.

"Oh my goodness!" Soonie had squealed.

"Shhhhh," Zillia looked around at the other family members in the room. "No one else but Wylder knows. But isn't it wonderful?"

Good thing for Uncle Isak I'd already committed to come, otherwise the sheriff himself wouldn't have been able to drag me away. Soonie swirled her feet in the water, watching tiny bubbles form on the surface. Riding away from her home and family had been the hardest thing she'd ever done.

The day she left, tears had rolled down her grandma's wrinkled cheeks, and new creases formed in the corners of her grandpa's faded blue eyes. Wylder's jaw was set in the hard line that only showed when he was most upset. They respected her choice to go, but all feared for her safety.

How would they have felt to see me hiding out on the hill? Soonie closed her eyes.

The waves of sadness coursing through her were soothed by surges of peace. This journey was right and true, and she needed to go. When Uncle Isak had asked her to come and be a teacher for the children, she had felt a tug in her spirit. Reassurance grew stronger every day.

"Susannah," Bright Flower called from further down. "Come, fish with us."

"I'll be right there." Soonie pulled her feet from the water. She led Stone Brother back to the other horses so he could join them for a supper of river grass.

She crept down the bank, avoiding the slippery moss and wet patches on the rocks.

Tersa held out a cane pole. "Here." She pointed to a rock. "You sit in this place."

Soonie obediently sat, drawing her knees up and pulling her skirt over them.

In childhood, grandma sent her and Wylder down the river to fish all the time. Since Soonie's nephews had come to live with them four years ago, she hadn't needed to go.

Beside the rock was a soft patch of mud. She found a worm, baited the hook, and threw the string into the water.

Tersa and Bright Flower nodded, smiled and moved to different areas on the bank. Soon the three women were fishing in contentment, lost in their own thoughts.

Only a few quiet moments passed before Tersa leapt to her feet. Her pole bent towards the water, and a silvery creature thrashed madly in the shallows.

In her excitement, Soonie dropped her own pole. It slid into the water, and she caught it just before it was lost. *I forgot how fun this is.*

Tersa gave a mighty tug and a handsome bass flopped onto the rock, mouth agape. With an expert flick of a slender brown hand she sent the fish into a basket.

Every gesture was filled with grace and purpose. It sparked Soonie's vague memories of her mother, who had been half Comanche. The simplest task had been beautiful to behold, and each moment held a dance.

More time passed, and Soonie's eyes became heavy. She pinched her arm to stay awake, watching the skin change from pink to light brown again.

Then a tug ran through the line and into her hand, a jolt like the electric shock from the machine on a traveling salesman's wagon.

The line slackened while the fish moved closer to the bank, invisible beneath the smooth surface of the water. Then the jerks became harder and more urgent.

She pulled the cane pole, hand over hand. At the end of the pole, she began twisting the line around her fist. Finally, the glistening fish broke the surface and swung into the air, almost smacking her in the face.

Tersa pulled in her line and began to walk towards Soonie, but Bright Flower shook her head.

Soonie grasped the fish beneath the gills with one hand, removed the hook, and walked over to sling the fish into the basket.

Tersa and Bright Flower both nodded and returned to their poles.

After supper had been consumed and the fish bones buried to prevent unwelcome visits from wild creatures, Soonie settled onto her blanket to watch the fire.

"To stare into the fire is to blind one's self to one's enemy." Uncle Isak sank down beside her, his movements soundless as an owl's flight.

Soonie blinked. "I have no enemies." But she tipped her head back. Stars appeared one by one, winking as though angels lit candles in the darkness. Fewer trees dotted the landscape in this area, and the sky seemed bigger and closer than ever before.

Uncle Isak bowed his head. "Ah, Little One. Your life has been one of shelter and peace, in a world of rare acceptance. I have already described the place where we are going. We have chosen to live free of the reservation and the white man's rules. But that freedom comes with great price."

"Will the people accept me?" Soonie glanced at her arm, close to Uncle Isak's. Even in the dim light, the contrast of skin color was apparent.

Uncle Isak picked up a twisted stick and pulled a knife from his belt. He began to remove the bark in smooth curls. "The settlement has many people like us, some Comanche, some Kiowa, and a few like you and I, with blood from different worlds dripped into the same bodies. All believe in our people, in our survival. The children must learn to read and write, to have the same abilities as those who would rule over us with white fists. They must learn mathematics so they can understand contracts and bills of sale, so they will know what they are agreeing to before they sign."

His turquoise eyes flashed black in the firelight. "At the reservation in Fort Sill, the older ones were educated by white men. But we are separated. We have asked you to come because you respect the people, and our ways, and you possess the gift to teach. Though the Comanche and Kiowa's world is destroyed, we must move forward and live on."

Soonie rested her chin in her hands. "Do you think they will learn from me?"

Uncle Isak shrugged. "You must make them listen."

I wish it were as simple as that. Soonie poked at the fire with a stick. Her teaching certificate, still crisp, was folded inside the cover of the small Bible Wylder and Zillia had given her as a going-away present.

Uncle Isak went to speak with the other men, and Soonie found herself staring into the fire once more. Soon, fatigue won over her fascination with the dancing flames. She spread her blanket beside the sleeping Tersa and stretched out.

Bushes surrounding their camp rustled, and normal night noises were broken by the startled cries of small creatures who suddenly found themselves claimed as dinner.

Lord, I am a stranger in a strange land. Give me wisdom. Let me have patience. Most of all, fill me with love."

One more prayer escaped her mind before she drifted off to sleep. *And never let me be afraid to enjoy a fire.*

2
Lone Warrior

"We will be home today," Bright Flower promised.

Soonie could scarcely believe it. Plodding hooves, scavenged meals and the constant stink of horse and sweat would soon be in the past.

Skirting around towns to avoid hostile encounters had not only made the trip longer, it also left them with few places to wash. Streams and ponds replaced pumps and baths. Though Soonie was used to wilderness living, she missed her Colorado River, which she had always followed, never more than a few miles from the banks.

The horses in front of her slowed, then halted on a ridge. Uncle Isak shaded his eyes and looked down over the rutted dirt road, which stretched before them like an endless brown ribbon. "Our place is a two hour journey from here."

"How have you remained hidden there for four years?" Soonie asked.

"Captain Wilkerson, in the fort nearby, has good reason to cover for us when trappers and prospectors get too close. The nearest town is five hours away, so there aren't many people in the area."

The captain risks his own position and freedom to protect a group of Comanches? More questions fought to escape Soonie's lips, but she held them back. Talking slowed the pace, and she trusted Uncle Isak. *He must believe we are safe, or he wouldn't have brought me here.*

Settling back into the saddle, she tried to move with the jolts to make them less painful. The path here was rougher than any of the roads encountered thus far. A wagon driver would need great skill to make it through this pass.

Bluffs with crumbling edges, like slices of cake, rose up on either side of them. The ground began to slope so much Soonie worried the horses might lose their footing. No one else seemed to share her concern, so she allowed smaller matters to overtake her thoughts.

"Will there be a stream or pond where I can wash before we reach the settlement?" she asked Tersa, who was now riding beside her.

The woman's dark eyebrows drew together. "Wash? Why?"

Soonie held out her arms, where streams of sweat mixed with dirt made crooked patterns on the skin. "I'm filthy, and I smell terrible."

Tersa sniffed around her. "You smell fine."

The Comanche men always slathered pungent grease on their skin before they set out to hunt. Soonie supposed this was to mask their scent from prey. Clearly, this group had a different idea of acceptable odors.

I love these people--but I would give my new riding breeches for a place to wash.

Wind Catcher brought his horse to a halt, though Soonie had not seen him signal to the animal in any way. Every muscle in the horse and rider's body stopped cold, motionless as statues.

They appeared. No brush stirred, no rocks rolled onto the path. Three young men simply hadn't been visible before, and now were. They wore traditional fringed and beaded buckskin trousers. Two had Comanche-style braids, thick and falling far past their shoulders, like Uncle Isak.

The third man stood a head above everyone else, with a wiry, muscular build. His hair was braided loosely, and sharp spines were arranged in a sort of cap covering his head. *Porcupine quills.* Soonie sucked in a breath. She'd seen photographs of Kiowa people, and knew they shared the settlement with her Uncle, but she'd never met one. After the great wars, where they had fought beside the Comanche people as friends and allies, many moved with them to the reservation at Fort Sill, in the great Oklahoma territory to the north.

Uncle Isak moved forward and grasped one of the shorter men's shoulders. "My brothers, so good of you to meet us here."

The man with porcupine quills came to clasp hands as well, but his eyes traveled to Soonie's over Uncle Isak's shoulder and remained fixed on her face. Sparks flew from the dark pupils and threatened to singe her cheeks.

Before she could think, her fingers crept up to touch her warmed skin.

The man's mouth curved into a scornful smile through horizontal black stripes painted across his high cheekbones.

He must be one of the people who did not wish for me to be here. She lifted her chin and returned his stare. *I can't be mindful of those who stand against me. I have to move forward and trust God to arrange my path.*

Isak turned and held out his arm to her. "Lone Warrior, this is my niece, Susannah Eckhart. Soonie, Lone Warrior is the son of Brave Storm, the other leader of our settlement." He gestured to the other two young men. "Gray Fox and Thomas."

Soonie dismounted and moved toward the men, hoping they couldn't see how badly her legs were shaking. She held out her hand. "So nice to meet you. Please, call me Soonie."

The three men stared at her hand for far too long before she dropped it to her side.

Uncle Isak cleared his throat. "Hmmm. Well, as you know, Soonie came a long way to help our children, and I would like to get home so we all can rest."

Lone Warrior's mouth appeared to be set in a permanent line. Soonie blinked when he spoke. "Father has agreed to this, and the old men have agreed to this. It seems the young men have no say."

Uncle Isak's back stiffened. "We listened to you speak, despite your youth. Someday, the decisions will be left in your hands. But the elders have decided our children must learn the white man's ways."

Lone Warrior turned to Soonie, and his porcupine quills seemed to bristle even more. "So your answer is to bring this white woman . . ." he spat the words, "into our camp? So she can betray us all?"

Isak folded his arms and stepped forward, but Soonie could hold back no longer. "My mother was Isak's sister." She fought hard to keep the anger from her voice, for she knew it would only fuel a very strong fire. "She taught me to love our people. I have come here to help you." To her horror, angry tears stung the corners of her eyes. She rarely lost control like this. *But I'm so tired . . . and dirty.*

"So, Su-san-nah, you have come to teach." Another smile, cold and hard, broke over Lone Warrior's face. "Perhaps you should first learn to show respect."

"I am every bit as worthy as you." Soonie met his gaze. "We are all equal under God."

Gray Fox threw out a hand as if to strike her, but Uncle Isak moved forward and grabbed his arm before the blow could land. "You will not harm this woman. She is my honored guest."

"Is this what she will teach? Our women to be insolent? The children to speak back to their elders?" Lone Warrior shook his head. He jerked his chin, and the three young men melted into the woods once more.

"You're doing a pretty good job of that already," Uncle Isak said to the now still bushes. Soonie and Uncle Isak remounted their horses.

The other three members of the traveling group smiled grimly, but no one mentioned the heated exchange. They all started forward.

"I don't think I like him very much," Soonie murmured to Uncle Isak.

"Lone Warrior is a good man. But he did not live in the times I have seen, where war cries filled the air and the ground was littered with corpses, both white and

Comanche. But Lone Warrior's heart beats strong. I do not know a braver man."

He could learn some manners. Soonie hunched down in the saddle and kept her dark thoughts to herself.

In a short time, a dark shape appeared against the hills. At first, it looked like a structure Soonie's nephews, Will and Henry, might have created with river rocks.

As they rode closer, Soonie picked out details in the rock fortress. Small, crudely formed windows with iron bars over them, the rough texture of rock walls, scalded white from the sun. A soldier slumped against the gate, flicking his hand at flies and pulling his short-brimmed military cap down to shade his face.

Soonie's father, Charles Eckhart, had been a soldier at such a fort. Her mother, Lucy, had met him when he'd come to the reservation at Fort Sill on a supply run, and they had fallen in love. After his service, he convinced her to come down to Bastrop and live with his Swedish family, who welcomed her with love and acceptance.

What would have happened if my parents had chosen to stay by the reservation? Would they have ended up at the settlement, in hiding? Would their eyes slant sideways at every sudden noise?

The guard stood up straight when they rode past. His brightly polished buttons shone on the dark blue fabric of his coat. "Mr. Isak, how are you today?"

"Fine, Lieutenant Ford." Uncle Isak nodded back. He dismounted and shook the man's hand.

"Is she a new one?" The guard stepped closer and studied Soonie as though she were some mysterious creature from the woods. "I don't remember seeing her here." His face was smooth and pale, blond whiskers just barely growing in. His gaze was not hostile like Lone Warrior's had been, merely curious.

"My niece, Susannah Eckhart," Uncle Isak replied.

Soonie slid to the ground with as much grace as she could muster, and swept the man her nicest curtsy, learned from Zillia's mother years ago. "Lieutenant Ford, so nice to meet you."

The young guard's eyebrows traveled to the brim of his cap. He took the hand she offered him. "The pleasure is mine, Ma'am."

"I apologize for the state I'm in. Eight days is an awfully long time to be on horseback."

"Yes, it would be. We don't have any womenfolks here, so the men can get pretty ripe themselves."

Uncle Isak cleared his throat. "We'll be on our way now, Lieutenant Ford, if there are no further questions." Soonie wasn't sure if the glimmer in his eyes was from annoyance or amusement.

"Lone Warrior and his friends were here a little while ago, wearing their paint," Lieutenant Ford called as they walked back to the horses.

Uncle Isak snapped around. "Yes, they came to meet us to make sure we had arrived safely."

The young man's cheeks reddened. "Well, uh, Mr. Isak, sir. I reminded him about the paint. My captain worries when those young braves travel the roads like that. Not to mention they scared the blazes out of me."

The group on horseback folded their arms and glared at Lieutenant Ford.

A lump rose in Soonie's throat.

Uncle Isak's face clouded, but he answered the young soldier in a level tone. "As I have explained to Captain Wilkerson, Comanche and Kiowa men wear paint for many different reasons. The hunting parties avoid the main road and in four years have never been seen. The paint does not signify war, it is simply a part of who we are, which is one of the reasons we came here. We should be free to express that tradition."

Lieutenant Ford nudged a rock with a booted toe. "Yes, sir. Just thought I would mention the captain's concerns." He looked up, and Soonie saw the glint of intelligence his hat had been hiding. "I know black paint stands for war, Mr. Isak. Don't know why they have to choose that color."

Soonie's uncle bowed his head. "I don't think they truly know, either, Lieutenant. Thank you for bringing it up. I'll speak to your captain about the matter."

The guard went to open the gate.

Uncle Isak raised his hand. "Another time. We are tired and hot and our horses are weary. We will go on for now."

Lieutenant Ford opened his mouth, darted another look at Soonie, closed it and nodded. "Yes, sir, Mr. Isak. I'll tell Captain Wilkerson to expect a visit from you soon."

"You go right ahead." Isak mounted his horse and waited for Soonie to follow suit. They continued down the path.

A little past the fort, the horses crested a high bluff. Uncle Isak gestured toward the rock wall. "The settlement is right around the corner."

A flutter of excitement filled Soonie's heart. Beyond lived a family she hadn't met, traditions and cultures she had longed to explore, and her new home.

3
The Settlement

Smoke drifted in lazy threads over the ridge line. Soonie asked Wind Catcher, "Won't someone guess the settlement is there if they see the smoke?"

The middle-aged man shrugged. "Very few strangers come here. Lone Warrior, Gray Fox and Thomas scout the roads, watching for travelers. Fires are kept small during the day."

Round hills covered in sun-browned grass rose from the earth, looking like mottled pigeons with heads tucked beneath their wings. The horses plodded through a valley creased between the mounds. On the bluff's other side, the settlement unfolded.

Giant, cone-shaped tipis squatted haphazardly along a wide, bowl-shaped surface of rock, fringed by cedar trees. To the east was a clearing, with a circle formed of boulders. Behind the bowl a jagged cliff rose up. Homes of mud and wood sat on shelves in the hillside, along with gardens. A path snaked through the structures.

Uncle Isak moved past the settlement before Soonie's curious eyes had time to study everything. He led the group down a path that skirted through trees to a wide, grassy area. Here was a log corral, with several other horses grazing within its fences. Uncle Isak flung out an arm. "Stone Brother's new home."

Soonie quickly dismounted and pulled the saddle off her weary horse. Tremors went through the animal's skin as flies buzzed and landed, and he tossed his head.

"You finally get a rest, dear one," she whispered. She reached in her carpetbag for an apple, the last one from a bag from Grandma. "Enjoy it, I don't know when you'll get another." she told him as he crunched it between giant yellow teeth. Juice dribbled down his velvety lips.

She joined the other riders in rubbing down the animals and checking their hooves for cracks and stones.

Uncle Isak gestured to the camp. "Everyone will be out to meet you soon."

Soonie shaded her eyes to study the distant tipis and buildings. "I'm a bit confused. I thought the Comanche and Kiowa people didn't build anything but tipis."

"On the reservation, some do live in structures made with government supplies," said Uncle Isak. "The chief, Quanah Parker, owns a very large wooden home. But our people did not build these shanties. Prospectors set up this camp many years ago, after a silver vein was discovered. They mined for a short time but didn't find much, so they went away."

"And no one else comes here?"

Uncle Isak chuckled. "Captain Wilkerson took care of that. His soldiers spread stories of ghosts and evil spirits haunting these hills. The tales are so terrifying they even scare me, though rattlesnakes pose a much more realistic danger."

Soonie nodded. Superstitions ran rampant in Bastrop as well. If a place held even the hint of a ghost, townsfolks avoided going there at all costs.

"Another reason no one has tried to settle here is because of floods. The houses on the hills are safe, but we've had to move our tents several times to keep them from being washed away." Uncle Isak shook out his saddle blanket and folded it. "The floods bring blessings in addition to troubles. Our gardens grow in the rich soil brought in by the waters."

Uncle Isak opened the gate for the horses to enter, and then closed it behind the swishing tails. He nodded towards Soonie. "Are you ready to meet everyone?"

Soonie smoothed out the wrinkles in her blouse. The flowered pattern was all but obscured by dust and grime. She glanced at the horse trough. If she splashed water over her dirty face, it would only create a muddy cascade. *It's no use.* She gave Uncle Isak what she hoped was a brave smile. "Lead the way."

The noon sun spilled over the rocky bluff in a waterfall of light. People began to move out of shadows cast by the houses and tipis. They shaded their eyes as they looked toward the group by the corral. On the other side of the valley, carts filled with vegetables rumbled through an opening in the wall.

"The building over there," Uncle Isak pointed to a large log hut, under a group of trees, "will be your school house. It also serves as a church when the traveling preacher comes through."

"Do all in the community believe in Christ?" Soonie asked.

Uncle Isak's eyes narrowed. "No, Little One. About half of the people are believers. But we have learned to accept each other's different faiths. Everyone should be free to follow their own beliefs."

Cries of excitement filled Soonie's ears as children of assorted sizes flocked towards her.

The little girls were clothed mostly in buckskin dresses and long, fringed shawls, though a few had town-style calico frocks. The boys wore trousers so faded and discolored it was hard to tell what fabric they were made from. Most of the boys were bare-chested and none of the children wore shoes.

A few children stopped to greet family members from the traveling group, but many surrounded Soonie, clinging to her skirts and pulling at her fingers. She smiled down into the faces. Several were dark as river earth; some were lightly tanned like her own. Pairs of golden, blue, and deep brown eyes stared back at her. Soonie fell in love with them instantly.

Their questions peppered the air like buckshot.

"Isak said to call you Miss Eckhart. Why?"

"Did you bring fancy white-people things?" asked a girl of about ten, who wore the cleanest dress and had the whitest collar. She eyed Soonie's traveling bag hopefully.

"I did bring a few items you might like. I will show them to you as soon as I get settled."

The girl clapped her hands. "I'm so glad you have come!"

"I'm happy to be here as well," Soonie said. Her heart warmed to its very core.

The adults stood back with folded arms. Most were older, a few looked to be the same age as Grandpa and Grandma. A group of teenage boys sulked over to the side. Porcupine Quills, as she had begun to call Lone Warrior in her head, and his two friends were nowhere to be seen. *I shouldn't be so uncharitable. After all, he has good reason to be suspicious. But he could have been a little nicer.*

A young woman with friendly eyes came up and gently parted a way through the children. "Laura, Little Boar, give Miss Eckhart room to pass. She will have plenty of time to answer questions later. The road was long, and she must be tired. Mira, Loud Raven, let's move over here."

The children all stepped back, still beaming.

"So nice you have come." The young woman patted her hand. "I am Molly. You will be staying with me and my grandmother."

"Thank you." Soonie surveyed the sea of children, who had all quieted. "Let me wash up and get some rest, and tomorrow I'll be out with the sunshine. I want to learn your names, but I'm so tired right now I wouldn't possibly remember them in the morning."

Molly threw her fringed shawl over a thin arm. Her umber hair swung freely, cut short like the other women's.

Soonie fingered her long, brown braid. *Maybe I should make a change. It would be much easier to care for out here.*

"Come with me." Molly led her across the clearing and up the meandering path. This was nothing more than a deep furrow in the hardened earth, with tufts of bramble and bushes sticking up alongside it.

"Your uncle asked if my grandmother and I would allow you to stay in our home. I was happy, because there are no other girls my age in the settlement. All the other women have children and are far too busy to pay me any mind, a widowed girl who knows nothing of their world."

Soonie stopped short. "You were married?"

Molly nodded. "Yes, three years ago."

"Goodness! You look so young. How old were you?"

"Fourteen. Many Comanche girls marry younger, but I was an orphan, and had nothing to offer but myself." She twisted a strand of hair around her finger. "My husband died of pneumonia a few months after the wedding."

"Oh, I'm so sorry."

Molly shrugged. "He was a good man, but I did not know him well, and felt no love for him. Grandmother Eagle wished for me to find another, but I am content on my own."

"Girls don't usually get married until sixteen or eighteen where I'm from," said Soonie. "But I think everyone was starting to worry about me, especially since my best friend got hitched, and I didn't have any prospects."

Though Soonie and Zillia had been friends since childhood, she'd noticed a change in their relationship since the wedding. Her best friend always put on a bit of an air when she talked about 'my husband' or 'my marriage.' *Perhaps I perceived a smugness that wasn't there.* Whatever the truth, she understood how Molly felt. Married women were simply *other*.

"What are these trenches, running beside the path?" Soonie asked Molly.

"They keep the water from the homes so they won't be washed down by the rain. Most of the water goes into the gardens."

"Wise prospectors." Soonie squinted up the hill. "But why would they put so much thought and hard work into gardening?"

"We dug the trenches," Molly said. "Did Uncle Isak tell you about Lone Warrior? He built the water way."

"Yes, I met him on the road." Soonie's grip on the handle of her carpet bag tightened. "He did not seem to want me here."

Molly shrugged. "He is a wild man. Sometimes I think Lone Warrior is an old soul in a new body. He may burst from his anger, like the wineskins."

"The old wine in the new wineskins? Have you read the Bible?" Soonie's heart leapt. *Could my new home belong to those who believe the same way I do? It would make this transition so much easier.*

"Yes, and I believe its words. I have given my heart to the true Creator." Molly's smile wavered. "But Grandmother Eagle does not. She is the Eagle Doctor of the tribe. She puts her faith in spirit animals, in Comanche herbs and magic."

The two girls reached the door of a small home. Whitewashed sides gleamed in the orange rays of the setting sun.

Molly tugged on the handle and placed a finger on her lips. "Shhh. Grandmother may be napping."

Soonie followed Molly into the house. A strange odor hung in the air, much like her grandpa's tobacco back home but with a stronger, earthier scent.

Two small windows let in slotted sunlight. Even after Soonie's eyes adjusted to the dim light, she could only pick out vague shapes. Perhaps that was a table over there, with pots stacked neatly on the wooden surface. The glow catching her eye must be a stove.

The darkness was interrupted by a spark as Molly struck a flint. It turned into a bigger glow when she lit a lantern's wick, which spread out to reveal colors and textures in the light.

Larger pots lined the walls. Above them were shelves filled with jars, skins. *And books?* Almost as many books as the schoolhouse back home. All shapes and sizes, at least two dozen. They seemed out of place in the otherwise primitive home.

From a pile of blankets in the corner, smoke curled and created eerie shapes on the lantern light. The blankets shifted, and a wizened face, wrinkled as a peach pit, poked out at the girls. Tiny eyes, sunk deep in sockets, blinked.

Soonie stiffened and tried to smile.

"Grandmother, this is Susannah."

"I am honored to meet you." Soonie held out her hand. The beady eyes regarded her hand, and looked away. *I need to find a new way to greet people.*

"She has traveled far. May I show her our room?"

Soonie had all but forgotten the carpet bag, gripped in her hands, though it had banged her knees all the way up the hill. Lowering the bag to the floor she rubbed her fingers together, trying to coax feeling back into them.

In the close quarters, the stench coming from Soonie's own self was horrendous. *I shall vomit if I have to stand here much longer. These poor ladies, I'm surprised they aren't begging me to wash. Do they not notice?* A new idea struck her. *Perhaps they do notice, but are terribly polite.* The more she thought about this, the more she felt it was true.

Grandmother Eagle placed a corncob pipe between her cracked lips and puffed. Long, thin fingers removed the stem again and she stared at Soonie for a very long time. She finally spoke, mostly in Comanche, with a few English words peppered in. "You have the white man's faith, then, like Molly. It is as I've thought. The old ways will pass, the new ones will live. The white man will not rest until the old fires have burned out."

Soonie did not know what to say, so she remained quiet. The hairs on the back of her neck prickled. This feeling had only come over her a few times in her life. *It's like the Bible says. We fight not against flesh and blood, but against spirits and principalities.*

"What good will the lessons you bring be, girl?" the old woman continued in a voice as raspy and dry as last fall's leaves. "Since Molly could toddle along the path, I taught her the way of the eagle doctor. She would not listen. I spoke of the old and powerful magic from our forefather's dawn. She did not heed my words."

"New ideas are useful, Grandmother," Molly gestured toward the shelves. "My books have showed me many ways to help people."

Grandmother Eagle raised a gnarled hand. "Susannah does not wish to hear our squabbles. Take her to our room."

Molly dipped her head and beckoned to Soonie, who picked up her carpet bag once more. The younger girl led her through a side door. "You will sleep in here, with Grandmother and me."

The room was tiny, smaller than her grandma's pantry back home. Three small bunks lined the walls, with scarce space between the head of one and the footrest of the next. Neatly folded bundles of cloth were stacked on the floor in-between. More shelves sat at eye-level.

Molly pointed to an empty one. "This space is for you. I have a few things to do, but I'll return in a little while. Please, feel free to get settled." She went back to the kitchen.

Having once shared a tent at a lumber camp with three other women, Soonie was no stranger to small spaces. But the walls were so close, if she stood in the middle of the room and stretched out her arms, she could almost brush them with her fingertips. Tenderness tugged at her heart. These people had so little, and they were sharing it with her. *Even if Grandmother Eagle does not wish me to be here.*

It only took a short time to arrange her spare clothing, books, and keepsakes in their designated place. Weariness overwhelmed her, and she fought a sudden, inexplicable urge to curl up on the little cot and cry her eyes out.

"Come with me," Molly appeared at the door, white teeth shining in the dim light. "I've poured some hot water in the washbasin for you."

In the living area, a brightly woven blanket had been hung in the corner.

"Praise the Father," Soonie breathed, as she caught sight of steam creeping through the crack, like wispy fingers, beckoning her in.

The items she had longed for were waiting behind the blanket. A small washtub with water, an ancient scrubbing brush, and a lump of homemade soap. Bathing was much the same way back home, when she didn't go out to the woods to wash in the river.

The water swirled over her arms, and the weariness of the road washed off her shoulders.

On the other side of the blanket, an old hymn, sung in Molly's sweet voice, drifted from the cooking area. The song was answered by a raspy, rhythmic chant in the Comanche tongue.

Soonie stared at the ceiling, almost expecting to see the spirits waging battle above her head. *I can't see it, but I can feel it. God, please keep me strong in this divided home.*

4
Breakfast With Molly

Soonie's eyes fluttered open in the half-light of dawn. Even though her muscles had been overworked for years on the farm, she was not accustomed to days spent on horseback. Stifling a groan, she stood and dressed. The other beds were already empty, their woven blankets pulled tight and smooth.

No matter how early Soonie had woken at home, Grandma and Grandpa were always up before her, rocking by the fire in chairs brought all the way from Sweden. Wizened heads would be bent over Bibles, hands clasped in prayer.

The scent of fresh corn bread drifted into the room. Her stomach grumbled.

The new Bible was hidden beneath a few other keepsakes on the shelf. Pulling it out, she read a few verses in the dim light. She'd already read every page of her old Bible, but each time she picked up the book she would see something new, or a verse would speak to her in a different way. Grandpa had explained this when she was a little girl. "That's why the Bible is called the Living Word. Fresh revelation comes with each reading, because the Holy Spirit gives you understanding when you need it the most. The Holy Spirit is our advocate, our comfort, and our friend."

Grandpa didn't always go to church on Sunday, but he knew more about God and the Bible than any preacher Soonie had met. She figured he must wait for everyone else to trundle off in the buckboard on Sundays, and go into the woods to have his own sort of church.

Part of Soonie sympathized with this habit. She too felt closest to God while walking in the woods, or when she danced in a forest clearing. But she also enjoyed worship and fellowship with other believers.

A sharp pang hit her insides again, and this time it wasn't from hunger. She missed her family so much.

She brushed these thoughts away, along with a tear, and put her Bible back on the shelf. *This won't do at all. Not on my first day of school.*

Molly lit up when Soonie came into the main room. She gestured to a tin plate, where corn bread was already sopping up the broth from pinto beans. "Eat."

"It smells heavenly. Thank you so much." Soonie sank down on the folded blanket which served as a cushion. A quick glance around the room showed no sign of Grandmother Eagle.

Molly saw her looking. "Grandma is out in her herb garden."

"Oh. All right." Soonie bowed her head for a quick, silent prayer.

"You don't have to worry," Molly said when Soonie opened her eyes. "Grandmother and I respect each other's rituals."

What rituals does an Eagle Doctor practice?

Soonie's mind swept over her mother's stories, tales of bone dances and mystical chants and ancient curses, but she couldn't remember anything specific. She shuddered. Though wishing to learn more about her people, this was a rock she would rather leave unturned.

The beans rolled over her tongue, mealy and cooked just right, sweetened with a touch of molasses. A nibble of crisp cornbread went with them perfectly. Before she took another bite, she contemplated the spoon. "Where does the food you can't grow here come from?"

"Trade with the soldiers," Molly said.

Soonie gazed around the room at the colorful items hanging from hooks on the walls. "I remember Uncle Isak bringing some things down to trade. He never told us how dangerous it must have been for him. In fact, he didn't tell us about the settlement at all. Until he asked me to teach, I thought that's where he was, all this time. What do you barter here?"

Molly held out her wrist and shook a colorful bracelet. "We make jewelry and blankets. The soldiers at the fort pay us with food and tools, then sell the items in Dallas, or give them as gifts to family members and sweethearts back home. In the city, these things can be sold for more money, but we are happy with food and clothing. We don't need much."

Soonie examined the bright beads. "These are beautiful. Do you make them from rocks?"

"No. In this hill is a copse of clay. We form the beads from the earth, bake the shapes, and color them with paints made from minerals and plants."

"I have an old wampum belt from my mother, passed down through her family. I left it at home for my nephews to keep for me," Soonie said.

Molly twisted the bracelet's leather ends around her finger. "My mother died of tuberculosis when I was ten. Grandmother performed all the rituals, and said all the prayers. Nothing helped. She said the spirits wished for my mother to come and walk with them.

"After my mother took her last breath in so much pain and suffering, I decided to study white man's medicine." She clenched the bracelet in her fist. "I could not accept the Comanche answer."

Soonie reached out to still the trembling hand. "I lost my mother when I was six. She died of some kind of fever. No one knew what it was. The white doctor in town refused to treat her."

Soonie recognized the sorrow in Molly's eyes. A dull, throbbing ache that could be sharpened to a point with a single word or thought. "We have so much in common," she murmured.

"We are related, in a way." Molly stood and cleared the dishes from Soonie's breakfast. "My grandmother and your grandmother were husband-sisters."

Soonie forgot to protest about Molly cleaning her mess. "You mean--you mean your grandmother married my grandfather after my grandma died?"

"No!" Molly laughed. "You should see your eyes! They're wide as sinkholes in the field! No. Comanche tradition allows a man to marry more than one wife. So your mother and my mother were half-sisters."

Soonie swept a few remaining crumbs into her hand, rose and threw them into the stove. "I knew Comanches had this custom, but I didn't realize my own family members had been a part. Mother always told me grandmother was a God-fearing woman!"

Molly shrugged. "She probably didn't have a choice."

"Poor Grandmother," Soonie closed her eyes. *Did she even love her husband?* She had never thought to pity her grandmother, captured and adopted by the Kiowa when a mere infant, then sold to the Comanche at the age of eight. She had only envied her life of intrigue and adventure.

"Women don't have much say among our people." said Molly. "Except for Grandmother Eagle. As the Eagle Doctor, she holds the most honored place in the settlement. The Kiowa traditions are different. Their women used to own the houses, and sometimes even went to war. I think that has helped even things out a little here at camp."

"Lone Warrior doesn't seem to have respect for women," said Soonie.

Molly pursed her lips. "I wouldn't say he feels that way about all women, just outsiders. He lives with his father and brother. No women in their home."

Molly pulled a cloth from a shelf and spread it over her hand. "Our mothers were best friends. They painted this together."

The deerskin had been worked until it was soft and supple. Two women danced across the shawl, flowers marking their path.

"Oh, Molly, it's beautiful." Soonie knew the woman with the orange dress was her mother, by something in the painted smile and the twinkling eyes. And above her mother's head, a bird in flight. "Sparrow. That was her Comanche name."

"Yes." Molly carefully folded the cloth and put it back in its place. "And because our mothers were half-sisters that makes us cousins, of sorts."

"How wonderful! I thought Uncle Isak was my only relative here." Soonie gave Molly a quick hug. "I just wonder why my mother never told me about our grandmothers."

Molly dipped her head to the side. "Maybe some things were too painful to remember."

"Perhaps." Soonie looked around for water to pour into the dish bucket. "Let me help you finish cleaning up before I go."

"Don't worry about that today," said Molly. "School will start soon, and you will want to prepare your teaching room."

"I haven't even been to the school house yet. What else should I take with me?"

Molly shrugged. "I don't know. I haven't been to school since I was ten years old, at the reservation. I tried to teach some of the children their letters, but I didn't have much patience for it and grandmother needed me here."

After gathering a small stack of books in her shawl, Soonie stepped outside. The sky was golden with the freshly-bloomed day, and heat hadn't yet begun to shimmer from the ground.

Many women worked in the gardens and hauled water from the stream bubbling out of the rocks on the east side of the settlement. The gardens had to be watered in the cool of the morning, or the liquid would evaporate as soon as it touched the ground. Soonie saw beans, corn and pumpkins growing, along with many other vegetables.

Tersa was busy weeding in a melon patch beside a tipi.

"Hello." Soonie waved.

Soonie!" Tersa came over to the garden's edge. "School begins today?"

"Yes, I'm excited."

"My daughter will be there. I will be glad for her to learn."

"You have a daughter?" *Eight days traveling together. How did I not know?*

"Yes, yes, my daughter is Laura. You met her yesterday, along with the other children." She turned her head. "Laura, the teacher is here!"

A girl, the one Soonie remembered asking about 'white people treasures,' stepped out of the tipi. Her clothes were clean and crisp, hair combed and tied back with a ribbon. "Miss Eckhart," she breathed. "You came to my house?"

"Why don't you call me Miss Soonie? And would you like to walk to the schoolhouse with me?" Soonie asked.

"Let me get my lunch." The little girl ran back into the tent.

Tersa shook her head and smiled. "She has been so excited about you coming. I want her to learn. She knows how to read a little, but soon she will be able to read the Bible to us." Tersa clasped her hands together, creating a tiny shower of dirt.

Soonie hadn't considered the added benefits to the adults of the tribe. *Perhaps I can teach some of the older people as well, if they'd like to learn.*

Laura came back, with a small satchel in her hand. "I have bread for everyone, for lunch."

"I'm sure it will be delicious."

They walked to the schoolhouse. Laura darted a glance at Soonie's bag, but didn't say anything.

'Oh, yes, I promised to show you."

Soonie pulled out an oval locket, the silver tarnished and scratched. She opened it to reveal two photographs, one in each half. "These pictures are of my mother and father. Aren't they lovely?"

"They must miss you." Laura touched the locket with a trembling finger.

"They are both gone to Heaven now. This locket is the most precious thing I own." Soonie fastened it around her neck. "Here is something else belonging to my mother. A wedding present from my father." She unwrapped a small piece of flannel to reveal a silver comb, with three dark garnets that shone like drops of wild grape jam.

"Oh," was all Laura could say.

"And I was going to save these for the classroom, but I'll give you one now." Soonie pulled out a peppermint stick. "I have a piece for each student."

Laura's eyes grew round as she took the treat. "This is to eat?"

"Of course. It's candy."

"I've never had candy." Laura broke off a small piece and put it in her mouth. "It's so good, Miss Eckhart!"

The joy on the little girl's face made Soonie wish she had bushels of treats.

I must give them bushels of knowledge instead. Lord, please help me with this task.

5
School and Clay

"Onward Christian Soldiers,
Marching as to war,
With a cross of Jesus,
Going on before . . ."

The words of the song bounced off the cracked stucco walls of the large meeting house. Soonie waved a stick she had picked up from the ground on the way in a brave attempt to keep some kind of rhythm.

The younger children sang with out-of-tune exuberance, while the four oldest boys leaned against the wall with tight-lipped stares.

After the last note, Soonie held up her twig. "Well, children, I didn't think you would already know that song. We only began singing it at my church a few months ago."

The young ones beamed. Every small face had been scrubbed until it glowed, though some cheeks and foreheads were painted with lines and swirls. Soonie was thankful everyone was fully clothed.

"Perhaps we will try a new song tomorrow. Now, everyone have a seat." She gestured to the eight woven straw mats arranged on the floor in the corner of the room. "Timothy, you and the older boys will sit in the back."

Timothy, Lone Warrior's fourteen-year-old brother, slouched to the mat and sat down hard. His friends, Black Turtle, who was also Kiowa, and Hershel and Felix, who were Comanche, followed suit. Four pairs of eyes glowered at her.

"All right. Laura and Prairie Bird, you sit here, in the middle, and Mira and Little Boar, you get to sit in the front."

Everyone scrambled to their places.

When the room quieted, Soonie spoke. "First of all, how many of you know how to read and write?"

Everyone raised their hands, except for Mira and Little Boar.

Soonie couldn't hold back her astonished grin. "That's wonderful!"

Black Turtle snorted. "We had school at the reservation. We're not idiots."

"I would never suggest such a thing, Black Turtle. I only wish to find out what you have learned so I don't teach you things you already know. And from now on, please raise your hand if you have something to say."

Soonie handed out flat, smooth pieces of wood and thumb-sized chunks of charcoal to each student. "Children, I know these are not going to be easy to use, but we will try to get slates very soon. I would like all of you who are able, to write your names. Both your Christian name and your other name, if you please."

Mira raised her hand. "What does a Christian name mean?"

Hershel rolled his eyes. "It means the name the preacher gave you when you were baptized, dummy."

"Hershel! We will not use demeaning words in this class." Soonie lifted her chin. *I have to earn their respect right now . . . otherwise they will never listen to me.*

She picked up a slab of wood from the shelf behind her, which was the only piece of furniture in the room. Using her own piece of charcoal, she scrawled an 'M' and a 'L' across the uneven surface.

I need to obtain better supplies. Soonie had asked Uncle Isak if they could purchase slates. He hadn't been certain. They'd have to run the idea by Brave Storm first. If he gave his approval, she could request an order from Captain Wilkerson.

Mira and Little Boar each held their charcoal tightly and stared at their boards. Soonie sat down in between them. "Here we go." She showed them her board. "You two can practice first letters today. Mira, yours looks like this." She pointed to the M.

A slab of board flew over Soonie's head and thudded against the wall, followed by a piece of charcoal, which exploded into black dust.

She leapt to her feet to face a stormy Timothy.

"Why do we need to be here?" he shouted. "We use hides and paints. These boards are maw p'ahle!"

Though Soonie didn't know Kiowa, she could tell the word was unsavory by the scowl on his face.

Three other boards flew against the wall, as Timothy's friends stood and joined him.

Soonie straightened her shoulders and looked Timothy in the eye. Her heart raced and she took a deep breath, swallowing her anger.

"How dare you?" she said in a quiet, even voice. "You will all come and pick up your slates. You will write your names ten times each. And you four will sit inside for recess today. Do not make me fetch your fathers."

She turned and strode to the front of the room. Picking up her Bible, she flipped through the pages, refusing to turn around.

After a very long silence, she heard the miraculous sound of feet scuffing across the floor, the slates being retrieved, and boys settling back into their places.

She turned to see the boys writing. Timothy was practically hacking into his wood with the charcoal, making deep ruts in the surface.

Should I correct him further? Best not to poke the bear, as Grandpa would say.

"Now." She smiled with all the courage she could muster. "I can see we will need a way to clean up all this coal dust. Any suggestions?"

By the fifth day, lessons moved more smoothly. The four boys remained sulky, but obedient. From what Soonie heard, they were used to running wild through the woods like wolf pups. None of their mothers were alive.

Laura glanced up from her work and smiled. The two older girls had been helpful and eager to learn.

The older boys called Soonie 'Mah-Tame-Mah,' which was Kiowa for teacher. The younger children called her 'Miss Su,' since 'Soonie' proved difficult for them to pronounce.

Soonie held up a slab of wood with the day's Bible verse. "Be angry and sin not, Ephesians 4:26"

She tried to choose short verses since the charcoal was proving harder to manage than she'd anticipated. She'd chosen a longer passage on Monday, and it had taken the students twenty minutes to write it out. Everyone--including her-- was covered in smudges by the end of each day.

Eight slates, one for each child. Surely that couldn't be so hard? She could have bought a slate for a few pennies from Bastrop's general store. A few bracelets or a blanket should pay for all they needed.

Her hand crept to her woven belt. Hidden underneath was a pouch containing two five-dollar gold coins, a parting gift from Grandpa. Emergency money in case she needed to travel back home. *But some could be used for new slates, if that is the only way.*

Laura raised her hand. "Miss Su, may I please go to the privy?"

"Of course you may," Soonie answered, ignoring the guffaws from the older boys seated to her left.

While Laura stood and made her way outside, Soonie turned to her little shelf of supplies. In addition to slates, some new books would be nice to have. Her Bible, a few of Molly's medical books, and a battered copy of Aesop's fables were all they had right now.

She flipped open the fable book to the children's favorite story, one about a fox who tricked a goat in order to escape from a well. The cunning creatures were highly respected by the people in the settlement, and the children fought over who got to read the tale.

Laura returned from outside and sank down to the floor, her cheeks rosy despite her dark skin.

"Why do we learn such things?" Timothy muttered. His eyes were lowered to his board, where his letters danced out in perfect script. Though he always wore a smirk or a scowl, his eyes burned with intelligence, and Soonie prayed daily for ways to break through the thick wall he had built.

"Timothy, please raise your hand if you wish to speak." Soonie smoothed her shirtwaist and tried to keep the tension from her voice.

He folded his arms and leaned against the wall, his charcoal stick clattering to the floor. "These verses are not useful to a Kiowa warrior. We read the sky, the animal tracks, the patterns in the wind. We do not need the white man's words, or his God."

"It is my understanding that your father does believe in God, Timothy. And the settlement's elders, including your father, wish for you to learn these lessons. I am here to make sure you get an education."

He leapt to his feet, the feathers in his hair sticking out at odd angles. "I will not listen to this teaching! I am Kiowa! I will not have a woman tell me what to do!" His chest heaved, and his eyes bored into hers, waiting for a reaction.

Soonie closed the book of fables. *Time for a new approach.* "Very well. Why don't you teach me something today?"

The other children gasped and murmured to each other.

One of Timothy's dark eyebrows arched up. "Teach you?"

"Yes. I've wanted to know where you find the minerals you use to make your paint," she touched a bright yellow circle, painted on Mira's cheek. "Where did you get these colors?"

"Clay!" Little Boar shouted. He clapped a hand over his mouth and raised his hand.

"Yes, Little Boar?" Soonie held back a giggle.

"Clay, Miss Su. We get it from the side of the hill."

"Very well." She turned to Timothy. "You will show the class where to find the clays."

His chin lowered into his chest. "The clay is only for women's work."

She opened her Bible again. "Fine. I'll find five more verses for you to write today."

Black Turtle raised his hand. "Miss Su, I will show you the clays."

"Let's go." Soonie put the book back on the shelf, and the children raced to the door, jostling and pulling at each other.

Timothy didn't move. He had slouched down further and his eyes were glittery slits.

"Come on," Soonie pointed to the door. "I'm not going to leave you in here by yourself and I don't want to bother your father today."

With a gusty sigh, he rose to his feet and slouched across the dirt floor, hands dangling at his sides.

The class followed Black Turtle, who headed down the path in graceful lopes.

Women paused from handiwork or gardening, and watched the impromptu parade with mystified expressions. Soonie smiled and waved.

They climbed over small hills and into a large crack in the rock, which opened into a rocky, open-air enclosure, about the width and length of the school house. A trickle of water divided the ground. The children stepped in to bathe dusty toes in the meandering current.

"Here, Miss Su." Prairie Bird pointed to the wall.

Over time, various types of clay and sand had washed through the valley. Bright red, yellow and orange dirt layered the cliff, like the fancy cakes ladies sometimes made for Bastrop Sunday luncheons.

Little Boar ran over and dusted sand into his hand from the wall. He dabbed a few drops of water into his palm, then expertly mixed the two elements. With one finger, he painted orange swirls and lines on his face. "See?"

"How lovely!" Soonie touched a finger to the orange and brushed it on the back of her hand.

Soon all the children were busily painting rocks, tree trunks and each other. The supply seemed endless, so Soonie didn't worry about the women being upset about waste.

Prairie Flower came over with a handful of red paint. "It's your turn, Miss Su."

Soonie couldn't say no to the little girl's hopeful smile. She closed her eyes and tried not to flinch while tiny fingers brushed paint over her eyes and cheeks.

"All done!" Mira, who had come to help, clapped her hands.

Soonie bent over the stream. A Comanche maiden with bright circles and stripes painted over her cheeks smiled back. *Such a different me.* Though she had worn her buckskins and shawl at home, she'd never felt this part of herself so strongly.

Laura tugged at Soonie's neat updo until her hair flowed loose and free over her shoulders. She braided it, and then poked in a dove's feather. "Your hair is too long," she scolded. "You still look like a little girl."

"Yes, I've decided to cut it, to about here." Soonie pointed to her shoulder. "What do you think?" A sudden silence made her look up.

The children stared at her. Smiles played around all their lips, even Timothy's. But they weren't mocking. *Could that be respect shining from their eyes?*

She brushed out her skirts, then rescued her shawl from the tree where she had hung it. "Thank you, everyone. I feel very special to have been shown such a wonderful place."

Silence still hung in the air, but the children weren't looking at her anymore. Their eyes were filled with . . . fear? Concern? She turned to see Lone Warrior, leaning against the clay wall.

Soonie hadn't seen him since her arrival a week ago.

His face was clean of paint. Thin eyebrows narrowed over a thin nose, shaped to a point. High cheekbones added to this portrait of angular strength. His shoulders bent slightly, as though they carried generations of frustration and anger.

Porcupine quills still quivered in his hair.

She opened her mouth to attempt some sort of greeting, but closed it. The look on his face was so severe, she couldn't even think of what to say.

"You are not one of us." Lone Warrior's words dripped with scorn. "Go home, white girl, and dress up like your own kind."

Unbidden tears smarted in her eyes. His assumption that she was being disrespectful of their culture struck her heart like a dull knife. *If only I knew the words to speak, to express how I feel.*

With her eyes, she begged him to understand.

His mouth softened for a mere instant. Then he shook his head, turned and stalked away.

"We think you are beautiful, Miss Su," Laura whispered.

The other children nodded, except for Timothy, who had suddenly become very busy stacking rocks by the stream.

Soonie pulled a handkerchief from her pocket, moistened it in the water and dabbed at her face. "We should probably clean up and get back to class. It's almost lunchtime."

That night, Soonie pulled out a precious sheet of paper and began her first letter home.

August 25th, 1890

Dear Zillia,

If you write to me, do not be concerned if you do not receive a reply for many months. Correspondence in this area is shaky at best.

How are Wylder and Orrie? Give them both my love.

I miss you and Bastrop and our quiet walks down by the river. We only have a small spring here. I can hear it now from the tiny, open air window in my room. It has a nice voice, but not the same as my own wild, rushing Colorado River. Daylight still flows in, though it is late. I will miss my light when winter comes, candles and lantern oil are dear here.

Oh Zillia, everything is so strange! I spend each night going over the events of the day again and again, wondering what I could have done better, or differently. So much is needed. Can I make a difference? Am I even up to this task?

Soonie paused and tapped her pencil against her lips. The week had been so much more difficult than she thought. But what fun they'd had with the clay!

She added a few more lines to her letter, then signed her name. *I will look for the bright spots in each day, and shine them up as best I can, like pennies sprinkled on the path. All I can do is my best.*

6
Sunday

One more twist.

SNAP!

Soonie stared at the broken halves of the metal hair pin in horror. The last of the five she had brought, and no way to purchase replacements. Perhaps Grandma Louise could send her a packet, but letters from the south were scarce. Any correspondence would come by rail, addressed to Captain Wilkerson to be picked up from the fort. *Better figure out a new way to arrange my hair.*

A bundle of thin rawhide strips lay on the shelf and she pulled one out of the pile. Twisting the sections of hair, she bound them into what she hoped looked like a respectable bun. Styling had become more difficult since she gave in to temptation and cut a foot off her braid, but the resulting coolness had been worth it.

Uncle Isak had told her a circuit preacher, Clance Jenkins, traveled a route between Dallas and Fort Sill every few months, preaching, baptizing and marrying couples along the way. A close friend of Uncle Isak's had mentioned the settlement to the preacher. He'd been riding there for over a year, risking a prison sentence if caught.

Soonie couldn't wait to meet him. *What a noble man he must be, willing to sacrifice so much to preach the word of God.*

Soonie smoothed out her crisp muslin pinafore, which covered a lilac-sprigged calico gown. She poked her head into the larger room. "Molly, would you mind helping me with my buttons?" No one answered, so she pushed through the door and into the living area.

Grandmother Eagle sat on her pile of blankets, tobacco smoke floating over her head. Though they lived in the same house and slept in the same room, the old woman rarely spoke. Soonie's attempts at polite conversation were almost always ignored. But today the aged eyes watched her intently.

The Comanche woman rose and hobbled over to her, reaching out a hand.

Soonie blinked, then smiled. She turned around and felt the pieces of her dress pulled together as the buttons were fastened one by one.

"You wear white woman clothes when the white preacher comes?" Grandmother Eagle's voice rasped, like a gate not often opened.

"Oh, that's not the reason I dressed like this. It's my custom to wear these kinds of clothes to church. I always have."

"It is fitting." Grandmother Eagle fastened the last button and went over to the table. Dried seed pods of some kind were spread out on its surface. She picked up a smooth, flat rock and began to pound them into dust. "White man's clothes for the white man's God."

Soonie raised her voice to be heard over the pounding. "But He's not just the God of white people. I don't know why some of you use this term. Jesus created all people, of every tribe, tongue and nation. He loves everyone the same."

"What language is your book?" Grandmother Eagle pointed to the Bible in Soonie's hands.

"English."

"White man's language, white man's God." Grandmother Eagle gathered the powder into a little pile, then poured it into a tin cup. She added a dipper's worth of water and handed it to Soonie. "There. Soothe your headache."

"How did you know I . . . "

Grandmother Eagle reached out and touched Soonie's forehead between her eyes. "Lines are here too soon for such a young girl."

"Well, thank you." Soonie peered into the cup, but knew better than to smell it. She'd experienced a few Comanche home remedies already. Downing the brown liquid in a gulp, she held back a grimace. *So bitter!*

The wizened little eyes never left her face. "At your church, you will feel better. Go have a good day with your God."

"I will. Won't you . . . won't you come with me?"

"Comanches do not need a God. We have our spirit animal guides, and our own minds to follow. Some say Peyote helps the men speak with God, but they are mistaken. We do not need anything more than what we already have inside."

Sadness enveloped Soonie like a sudden, soaking rain. How she wished she could be the one to help Grandmother Eagle see the truth. But she sensed the woman's spirit was shut tight like a steel trap.

Molly came in the door with an apron full of eggs. "Good morning." She went to the washbasin and wiped hay and dirt from the smooth, brown ovals before placing them in a box by the stove.

"I could have helped you gather these." Soonie touched one of the still-warm shells.

"You help me every morning," Molly answered. "My, don't you look beautiful." A hungry look swept over her face; one Soonie had caught a few times when she brought out something pretty from home. She pushed back her hair, which swung freely.

"Would you like me to put up your hair? It wouldn't take very long. I used to arrange my friend Zillia's hair all the time."

"No. I wouldn't want you to take the trouble. My hair's too short to fix." A flush crept up Molly's cheeks. The soft brown eyes darted over to Grandmother Eagle, who only grunted and went back to her pile of blankets.

"I can still make it look pretty. Mine isn't much longer than yours, now. Please. Let me." Soonie pulled the silver comb from a pocket, sat on the floor and gestured in front of her.

Molly giggled. "Oh, all right."

Soonie combed through the shoulder-length, glossy tresses with her fingers. All the women of the camp washed their hair with mint to keep away bugs. The herb gave a shine the women of Bastrop would have envied.

"I miss my hair," Soonie murmured while she braided and looped. "I'm going to let it grow again."

Molly shrugged. "Most of the women here don't have time to fix long hair, and it is our custom to cut it short. Only the men let it grow."

"It's the opposite where I'm from," said Soonie. "My grandmother would whip out her scissors any time the boys' hair passed their collars."

"Men here only cut their hair when in mourning." Molly played with a piece of leather tie, weaving it through her fingers. "Sometimes they even take hair the women have cut and use it to make their braids look fuller."

"Certainly different." Soonie parted sections of hair and began to braid them.

"My mother used to fix my hair for me," said Molly.

"Mine, too."

"She was young," Molly continued. "We told each other secrets. We were friends."

"I learned so many things from my mother." Soonie tied off the braid to one side and began on another. "Sometimes I wonder if she knew her life would be cut short." Lucy Eckhart, also known as Sparrow, had taken every possible opportunity to teach her children about their culture and heritage. Her mother had strained to hold on to the past, like someone who gripped the light of a dying sun.

"I think that will work nicely." Soonie finished the second braid.

"Thank you." Molly patted Soonie's handiwork and stood up. "We'd better go. All the best places get taken quickly." She shook out her skirt, which was made of rough-woven cloth like most of the other clothing in the settlement.

Soonie picked up her Bible and waved to Grandmother Eagle. "Have a nice morning. Thank you for helping me with my dress."

The woman grunted once more, but this time the corners of her wrinkled lips turned up slightly.

Outside, women rushed by with small children. Some greeted Soonie, but most simply hurried. All were dressed in their best and brightest, but no one else had anything as nice as Soonie.

"Are all the people who passed by Christians?" Soonie asked Molly. Almost everyone in the settlement seemed to be heading to church.

"Most. But some attend out of curiosity, or boredom. A few come just to keep an eye on the pastor, to make sure he's not spying on us."

Soonie stopped short and stared at Molly. "Do you think the pastor would do such a thing?"

Molly laughed. "Not Brother Jenkins."

Everyone entered the school house, which served for meetings when the months became cooler, and a church for rare visits from men of the cloth. True to Molly's prediction, the room was packed. Elderly men and women sat on the floor while the children and younger adults leaned against the walls.

A white man with a black coat and an ivory collar stood at the room's front, in the place she usually taught. His head was thrown back in song, his thick mane of brown hair sweeping the starched collar. He couldn't have been older than thirty.

After a quick scan of the wall, Soonie found a spot to stand. Sweat trickled down the back of her dress. Despite the cool September morning, the building was sweltering. She tried fanning herself with her Bible, but decided it might be disrespectful. Men and women turned to stare. *Why are they looking at me? Oh, it must be the way I'm dressed. Oh dear, I wasn't trying to bring attention to myself.*

In Bastrop, for many years she had insisted on wearing the Comanche style clothes her mother made for her. People had always stared and whispered when she came into town, but she'd never cared. *Why do I care so much now? This is part of who I am.*

Brother Jenkins finished the hymn and opened his eyes. He picked up a worn leather Bible from the bookshelf.

"Before I read today's Scripture, I want to make a note . . ." His voice trailed off as he caught Soonie's eye. He blinked and shook his head, then glanced up at her again.

Her cheeks grew hot as heads swiveled back to stare at her. She straightened her back and lifted her chin. *Surely I can't have done something so terribly wrong. I'm just wearing my church clothes. We are here to worship Jesus, not worry about our clothing.* She returned Brother Jenkins' stare with what she hoped was a cool look.

"Forgive me," he stammered to the congregation. "Let us open our Bibles to Romans 6:5-8."

"For if we have been planted together in the likeness of his death, we shall be also in the likeness of his resurrection:

Knowing this, that our old man is crucified with him, that the body of sin might be destroyed, that henceforth we should not serve sin.

For he that is dead is freed from sin.

Now if we be dead with Christ, we believe that we shall also live with him:

Knowing that Christ being raised from the dead dieth no more; death hath no power over him."

Brother Jenkins closed the Bible and stared into every eye before speaking. "Paul is saying, Christ has died for us, now we must die for Him. Death means putting away our old ways, our old manners." He pointed to a hide spread across the wall behind him, painted with a Kiowa hunting scene. "We must leave behind the old cultures, and embrace what is civilized."

Soonie put her hand over her mouth and looked around to see the people's reactions. All the faces were blank, as though resigned to whatever was brought before them. *Surely I am not understanding. I must have misheard.*

At Bastrop First Methodist Church, Soonie had listened to hundreds of sermons, given by the many pastors who rotated through the wooden doors, as well as guest speakers who came through town on occasion. But rarely had she seen one delivered with such gusto and spirit. Brother Jenkins pounded his Bible with a clenched fist and shouted with more zeal than a traveling salesmen. She soon lost track of the message completely, and by the closing hymn, she felt convicted, rattled, and slightly ill.

At the end came a long prayer, where Brother Jenkins prayed for "mercy upon this savage land and its peoples."

Is he implying my people are savages?

The congregation left the small building. Children yawned and adults fanned themselves.

Soonie headed up the path to her home to help Molly with the food they were contributing to the town feast in honor of Brother Jenkins. *I must hurry.* She was determined to have a word with the young preacher before he took his leave.

7
Brother Jenkins

A ring of large stones had been arranged in the center of the settlement. Councils were held there when the schoolhouse was too sweltering, along with storytelling nights, dances, and feasts which Molly described as rare and wonderful events.

Women spread bright blankets out over the largest stones. Children skipped in to arrange baskets and platters of food from their mothers' kitchens. Breads, roasted meat and corn sent heavenly aromas into the early fall air.

No one waited patiently in lines like the church functions back home. People crowded around the food, shoveling portions onto tin plates and scurrying back to family blankets.

Brother Jenkins was not among the mob. Scanning faces, Soonie saw him seated beneath the largest oak in town, in a rickety wooden chair someone must have brought out from one of the homes. It was the first chair she had seen since her arrival.

Wind pulled at his clothes and he attacked the food with the same exuberance used to deliver the sermon. His fork stopped half-way to his mouth when he caught her eye. With an almost ethereal wave of a thin hand, like the flutter of a dove's wing, he beckoned to her.

He's probably going give me a lecture on vanity. Oh well, I have a few issues with his ideals as well. Soonie picked up her skirts and marched over to his shady spot.

As she drew closer, Brother Jenkins placed his loaded plate of food to the side, stood, and bowed sharply. On closer inspection, everything about him was sharp. He had a sharp chin, cheekbones, and sharp shoulders on either side of a severely starched coat. Skin peeled beneath a light tan on every inch of visible skin, but his face was pale and pasty under a broad-brimmed minister's hat.

"I have discovered your name," he said, taking her hand. "You are Miss Susannah Eckhart." He stared at her palm, as though not sure quite what to do with it. Finally, he gave it a quick shake, and pushed it back towards her, like he was returning a package. With a shaky chuckle, he let go of her fingers.

"Yes, and you are Brother Jenkins." Soonie glanced around, but there was no one nearby to witness the awkward exchange. *This is absurd. I* will *gather myself.* "I—thank you for bringing the sermon today. It was very—enthusiastic."

"Trifle, trifle." He waved thin white fingers. "But you . . ." sharp gray eyes reached up to search her face. "Why would a white woman come all the way out here, into such danger? Mr. Isak said you were a school teacher?"

He certainly doesn't beat around the bush. "I am one-fourth Comanche," she said rather coldly. "Isak is my uncle."

"Extraordinary," the pastor breathed. "I wouldn't have thought . . . in those clothes. I mean, you don't look. . ."

"These are my church clothes," she said, like that explained everything.

"Oh. I see." His eyebrows knitted together above the long, sharp nose. "Say now, would you like to walk with me? It's cool out here today, and this is only my fourth visit to the settlement. I'd like to see more of it."

Soonie opened her mouth to refuse, then closed it again. *Perhaps I should give him a little more grace. After all, he is risking so much to bring his teaching ... even though I don't agree with his interpretation.*

"All right." She slipped her hand into the offered elbow. The absurdity of the situation was not lost to her as they strolled past gaping students. *Tomorrow I think we'll have a little lesson about the impoliteness of staring.*

Feet stepping high to avoid shuffling dust, they walked past tipis and homes, towards the paddocks.

A dozen horses grazed near the fence. They were long, lean beasts, used to wilderness life.

Stone Brother lifted his head, shook his golden mane, nickered and trotted up to the fence.

"Hello there, sweetheart." She stroked his velvety nose as he whiffed over her hand, searching for snacks. "I'm sorry, I didn't bring you anything."

Brother Jenkins stood back to watch the exchange. "Is he yours?"

She nodded. "Since I was fourteen. Uncle Isak brought him to me on one of his yearly visits." She pushed the horse away from her skirts as he nipped at her pinafore. "I never realized how dangerous those trips were for Uncle Isak, until now. It was so important for him to keep in touch with our family. He risked everything."

"Yes, yes, quite dangerous." Brother Jenkins threaded his fingers together and turned his back to the fence. "So you teach school, then?"

"Yes. I received my certificate last year."

"Surely other schools needed teachers."

A feather of irritation tickled the back of her mind. "I could have taught in my home town of Bastrop, if I wanted."

"Even though . . . they knew of your heritage, of course?"

Soonie swallowed and fought to keep her voice even. "My town, for the most part, accepted my brother and me. I never tried to hide my heritage. Either one of us could have worked wherever we wanted."

Brother Jenkins removed his hat and studied it intently, as though ancient inscriptions covered the brim. He flicked off a piece of lint and placed the hat back on his head. "You are very fortunate. Not all have found such a welcome."

"I know."

Brother Jenkins rubbed his chin. "It is only because of Captain Wilkerson's mercy this settlement is here at all. In my understanding, your uncle spared the captain's life during a battle twenty years ago."

"I have heard there was a reason, but no one has told me the full story."

"It's quite naive to assume your own safety without knowing the, ahem, full story, don't you think?" He must have caught the dismay on her face because his eyes softened. "Oh, but you are young. Your generation did not watch fathers march to war, never to return again, or see mothers shivering in homes, wondering about owl calls in the night. Well, here's the truth, Miss Eckhart. I can assure you if the elected officials in Austin or Washington D.C. had any notion of this settlement, you would all be driven out, and perhaps imprisoned."

Soonie pulled burrs from Stone Brother's mane, refusing to look at the preacher. "I fully realize that."

"Then why, Miss Susannah Eckhart, did you choose to throw your lot in with these natives?"

A lump formed in Soonie's throat but she choked it back and faced him, hands clenched at her sides. "I was called by God, Brother Jenkins, to be here for such a time as this. I don't know why I'm in this place, or how long I am to stay. But there is a reason. You understand what it means to be called, sir, I would daresay. When the still, small voice of your beloved Father God speaks to your heart, you are compelled to do whatever He asks."

Soonie's heart quickened, and she relaxed her fingers and wiped them on her skirt. She hadn't meant to react so strongly. Lone Warrior's angry face invaded her thoughts. What did he think of Brother Jenkins' visits to the settlement? *He's probably watching us right now.* Craning her neck, she studied the trees and bushes surrounding the corral.

"We can only surmise what our God wants from His holy scriptures," Brother Jenkins broke into her musings. "My family wanted me to be a minister, and so I pursued the cloth. As for why I am here, my district assigned me to Fort Sill. When I caught wind of the settlement, I felt it was my duty to shepherd these lost, pagan souls."

Every word pelted Soonie like a hailstone, and she stood frozen and at a loss for words.

The pastor glanced at the sky. "I have to leave soon in order to reach Fort Sill by sundown." His eyes slanted back to her. "We need all hands, working together, to bring the savage man to civility. I hope I can count on you to be of assistance."

On the way back to the settlement, Soonie's head swam with anger. She ignored Brother Jenkin's offered arm and kept her hands folded tightly into themselves.

After the walk, Soonie went back home intending to spend the rest of the day reading her Bible or in prayer. The pile of blankets was empty when she walked through the door. Once in her room, she settled down on her cot.

Closing her eyes, she opened her heart to the torrent of words pent up inside. "God, I don't know what to do about the preacher who has come. He says he serves you, but every word he speaks goes against what I feel in my heart. All men are created equal. You love us the same. God, please help me to know the truth. Give me confirmation that I am supposed to be here." As she prayed, breathing became easier, and her hands stopped trembling.

She took her Bible from the shelf and turned to Jeremiah 29:11.

"For I know the thoughts that I think toward you, saith the LORD, thoughts of peace, and not of evil, to give you an expected end."

A tiny shiver went down her spine. "Thank you God. Every time I need an answer, you always help me." She smiled wryly. *Even if it's not always exactly what I want it to be.*

The familiar peace and joy of the Holy Spirit flooded through her being, and she opened her heart to His presence. For a while, she lost all sense of time and place.

The bedroom door banged open. "Soonie, I've been looking everywhere for you!" Molly stepped in, a few wisps of hair fluttering around her face. Her hand crept to her mouth. "I'm sorry. I didn't mean to disturb your prayer time."

Soonie closed her Bible and smiled. "That's all right. Did you need something?"

"Yes. Come out and see. The people are having a game day in the field."

"On a Sunday?" Soonie frowned.

"Yes, yes. What's the matter?" Molly's eyes narrowed.

Soonie stood up. "Nothing. I keep forgetting how different things are here. I'll come."

They passed by the ring of stones, which was abandoned. Molly led Soonie down a path she hadn't seen before, through the trees until they reached a broad, clear field. People rushed around with sticks and colored scraps of material.

"Is Brother Jenkins still here?" asked Soonie. *Wonder what he'd have to say about this.*

"No, he left an hour ago. Come on over!" Molly gestured to Grandmother Eagle, who stood beneath a giant oak tree. The old woman wore a buckskin costume with fringed sleeves, covered with beaded designs of blue and white. Tiny shells had been sewn across the front.

Soonie had never seen the eagle doctor wear anything but a plain dress and shawl. The outfit emphasized her already regal, important persona.

"Susannah." The eagle doctor nodded in Soonie's direction.

"Grandmother, have they started yet?" Molly asked.

"They are coming." Grandmother Eagle pointed to the corral. The men were leading in the horses. Some steeds sported colorful painted handprints on their flanks, while others had circles and spots around their eyes. Many had feathers braided into their flowing manes. Every shining hair was in place, and Soonie suspected the men used the same herb to wash the horses as the women used for their own hair.

The men were splendid in their own right, with painted designs on their faces and arms. Some wore caps with porcupine quills or deer horns. Capes of woven grass were tied around many of the broad shoulders. In everyday life, Kiowa and Comanche men wore mostly the same kinds of clothes, but today the colors and patterns of costume were distinct for each group.

"What are they going to do?" Soonie whispered to Molly.

"First, they will ride." Molly's eyes shone, and she bounced on the balls of her feet. For an instant, Soonie saw the seventeen-year-old girl for who she truly was, apart from the tragedies and hardships that normally marked her beautiful face.

Soonie's jaw dropped as the men galloped past the spectators. Never had she seen such riding. The men's bodies moved with their beasts as though part of them, wild and perfect

Lone Warrior pressed to the front of the line. His ebony mare, Cactus Pear, pranced across the grass with dainty steps. His eyes met Soonie's, and her cheeks grew hot.

Why does that keep happening? She had a sudden desire to hide behind the tree. *I'm a grown woman, and I have every right to be here.* But her heart thudded in her chest in a way she had never experienced, like it was trying desperately to tell her something and she simply wouldn't listen.

She pressed her hand against the offending rhythm and focused her attention on the rest of the riders.

Grandmother Eagle stepped out before the line of halted horses and raised her hands to the sky.

"Why is she doing that?" Soonie whispered to Molly.

"She is blessing the day and asking the spirit guides to protect each horse and rider so they will not be injured during the contests," replied Molly.

After the blessing ended, Grandmother Eagle lowered her arms, and the horses surged down the field.

Molly tried to explain the contest as it went, but Soonie was quickly lost in the torrent of rules and traditions. The closest thing she could compare it to were the jousting tournaments from the knights of old.

Several women stood on the sidelines, holding long sticks with padded hides tied around the ends. A man would gallop by close enough to grab a stick, and then thunder after the other men, whooping and swinging the staff through the air.

Soonie decided the goal was to knock a rider off his horse. But this wasn't easily achieved. When a staff came towards a rider, he would slip down his horse on the other side, so the animal would shield him from the blow.

"And I thought I was a good rider," she said to Molly.

'This skill is passed down from the old to the young," said Molly. "It was first used during the wars, to hide from the arrows of an enemy."

If a man lost hold of his stick, a woman would dart into the arena, weave through the madness of sticks and hooves to pick it up, and run back to her spot to hold it out again. Soonie noticed that the women mostly helped their own husbands or family members.

"Who's on Lone Warrior's team?" Soonie hadn't seen him drop a stick.

"Gray Fox's mother is helping both of them." Molly pointed to an older woman, near the corner. "She doesn't run very fast. But they almost never drop their sticks."

As the game progressed, more and more men were knocked from their horses, which meant they had to leave the game. Soon, only Lone Warrior, Uncle Isak and Gray Fox were left.

Uncle Isak's smile flashed across the field as his horse gained on Cactus Pear. The beast's eyes rolled white and Uncle Isak swung his stick. Lone Warrior ducked in time, but his staff was knocked from his hand.

Gray Fox's mother stood with her mouth slightly opened, her hands clasped in front of her.

"She's too excited! She's forgotten his stick!" Molly said.

Soonie would never know what possessed her at that moment. Feet moved beneath her and she ran across the field, past Gray Fox, and retrieved the stick. She pressed it into the elderly woman's hands just as Lone Warrior thundered by to fetch it.

His eyes bore into Soonie's with a glint of . . . was it admiration? *Couldn't be.* Her breath came in short, quivery gasps.

Lone Warrior grabbed the stick and brandished it high in the air, throwing his head back to whoop. His knees tightened and Cactus Pear swung around.

So intent were the other two men on each other that neither noticed Lone Warrior as he bore down on them. He reached out to hook Uncle Isak's leg with the stick, flipping him off his horse. In the same movement, he nudged Gray Fox in the ribs and brought him down as well.

Both landed on the ground with thumps, like giant apples blown from a tree.

Everyone cheered while the two men stood up and dusted themselves off with sheepish smiles.

So much for a quiet Sunday. But Soonie had to admit, she wouldn't have missed it for twenty proper sermons.

8

Captain Wilkerson

Fall breezes ruffled Stone Brother's mane as he picked his way through the rocky path. Though the incline was gradual, recent rains had eroded the trail, making the trip slower than Soonie remembered from the month before.

She missed trees. The tallest bush in the pass was waist high, and only a few of the larger boulders offered a scrap of shade. *So unlike Bastrop's pine and oak forests.*

Uncle Isak's horse, Aruka, tawny like the deer she was named for, trotted ahead with sure steps.

Soonie patted Stone Brother's mane. "A few more months, and you'll be able to keep up with Aruka."

Uncle Isak had agreed with her about the slates right away, but it had taken many meetings and arguments to convince Brave Storm. Her uncle had given up hunting time and a long list of chores to ride with her to the fort.

The children were doing quite well considering they'd only had a month's worth of teaching and the limitations they faced. For the writing portions, they

THE COMANCHE GIRL'S PRAYER

moved to the shaded outdoors, to cipher letters with sticks in the fine sand. However, this only worked on days where the air was still. The slightest breeze could destroy an hour's work in seconds. When the rains came, they couldn't practice writing at all. *We need slates before winter, or I might as well not even be here.*

"Uncle Isak, could you tell me a little bit more about your friendship with Captain Wilkerson?" Soonie had meant to ask him for a while, but they had both been so busy she hadn't had a chance.

Uncle Isak's eyes grew hard, and he bowed his head. "It's not a story I like to tell."

His horse stepped ahead again, and for a section of trail he rode in silence, with his shoulders slumped.

Soonie urged Stone Brother alongside of his horse. "I'm sorry, Uncle."

He looked up quickly. "No, Little One, you deserve to know why we will always be safe if Captain Wilkerson is near us.

"I was a young brave, only twenty. This happened before you were born, before the world of the Comanche was limited to a few thousand acres in the Oklahoma Territory.

"Our group lived in tipis and moved where and when we wanted with no one to tell us otherwise. We considered ourselves unstoppable. Braves raided homes and outposts through Texas, stealing anything they could find. They acquired horses, goods, and even captive humans."

"You were part of that?" Soonie's stomach twisted. She hadn't realized Uncle Isak had been on raiding parties.

Uncle Isak frowned. "You have to understand, Soonie, I didn't follow Christ at that time, even though my mother tried to teach me. I grew up wild and free, and lived for the glory of the hunt.

"The chief saw my abilities, and I became one of the youngest men to lead my own band. Though we spread our share of mischief, we never killed except in self-defense. The men took horses right from under guards' noses." He chuckled. "My band of ten could clean out a stockade before a ranch hand could light a lantern."

Soonie smiled. Though she didn't condone the notion, it would have been fun to see the guards' faces.

Uncle Isak continued. "The white man's government knew they had to stop the Comanche. Settlers were terrified, and horses were stolen. Families, including little children, were killed, though never by the hands of my warriors. The president of the United States made a plan. He offered bounties on the head of every buffalo in the land. The buffalo were the life of the Comanche. In two years, almost all of the beasts were killed by hunters and left to rot in the sun."

Soonie knew this part of the story, but fresh sadness rolled from Uncle Isak in waves. "What a terrible way to destroy a nation," she murmured.

"Yes." The creases in Uncle Isak's forehead deepened. "My wife and child died of starvation while I was away. I thought there would be plenty of food. But everything was gone."

Soonie struggled to find a word or gesture to somehow ease the pain. "I'm so sorry, Uncle Isak."

He seemed to sink into himself for a moment, as though he wished he could become a part of his saddle, or horse, or some other emotionless object. "I have never experienced such loss, not with the deaths of all other family and friends. After I found out about my wife, I left my sisters and brothers and went to join Chief Quanah in the final war. I was given my own group to lead once more, and we were fierce fighters. No white man could stand before us, anger and grief strengthened each blow."

"One day, we encountered Captain Wilkerson's regiment. Winter was upon us, and we were all cold and hungry, but his men were not accustomed to dealing with the elements. They fought with valor, but soon bodies littered the ground, the whites outnumbering the Comanche dead two to one.

"I faced Captain Wilkerson. He had run out of bullets. My quiver was empty. We pulled out our knives and ran at each other, knowing this battle would be to the death. Drops of our blood mingled on the snowy ground.

"After a very long fight, I used a Comanche trick to trip him. I cared nothing for fair play, only lusted for the deaths of those who warred against my family. I held up my knife for the final blow.

"He stared into my eyes, and then closed his own. A look of peace covered his face. The man sighed and lay still.

"I realized at that moment, I wanted the peace he knew. Every bit of my heart was filled with sadness; pushing out the need for war and hate. I sheathed my knife, stepped back, and cried for retreat.

"All of my men stared at me. We had almost won the battle that day, and my band couldn't believe what they were hearing. But they trusted me, and followed my orders without question.

"Captain Wilkerson and his remaining men stood in the snow and watched us ride away."

"And he remembered you?"

"Yes. Five years later, when Chief Quanah ordered us to the reservation at Fort Sill; Captain Wilkerson was one of the men who fought for us to receive fair allotments of food and clothing. On the day we decided to leave, I found out where he was and we followed that path. He owed me a life-debt. At risk of his own military career and freedom, he's made good on that debt. Over time, we've built a friendship beyond that one day, and we both trust each other with our lives."

"What an incredible story," Soonie breathed.

The fort looked exactly the same as the first time Soonie had seen it, an undisturbed fortress on the plain. The guard who met them outside was tall and burly, with a scar running through his bushy, black beard.

"Howdy." Despite the friendly word, his tone was stern and his hand moved to his gun hilt.

"Hello. I don't believe we've met." Uncle Isak held out his hand.

The soldier kept hold of his gun. "Just came to this God-forsaken place last week." He looked them both over, and his eyes settled on Uncle Isak's knife, strapped in his waistband. "They said we had a pack 'o savages over yonder, and I don't like it. Don't know why it's allowed. Why don't you folks just move on?"

The muscles in Uncle Isak's cheek twitched. "The Captain happens to be a good friend of mine, and Miss Susannah here wishes to make a request of him."

Uncle Isak stood a little straighter, and his tone became more formal, like how the folks back home changed their mannerisms for church or a dance.

Loud creaking interrupted the exchange, and Lieutenant Ford stepped through the gate. A large grin spread over his face. "Miss Eckhart. Mr. Isak. What brings you here?"

The older guard didn't flinch. "The Captain really does know these folks?" he said incredulously.

"Of course." Lieutenant Ford bent close to the bearded man, speaking in a low tone. Soonie only caught the phrase, "saved his life."

He turned back to them and said in a louder voice, "They are as welcome as the Captain's own mother would be, not that she'd ever want to come out here." Lieutenant Ford opened the gate wider. "Come on in. Captain Wilkerson just finished breakfast. I'll let him know you're here."

Soonie had never been inside a military fort, but she found this one rather underwhelming. The front gate led to a path between two buildings. Once inside, she was greeted by several structures made from sun-bleached wood, positioned in a square around the larger command post. When Lieutenant Ford closed the gate, a cloud of dust filled the air. She sneezed.

Lieutenant Ford gestured to a heavy wooden door, set in the command post's wall. "If you folks will wait here, I'll go inside and make sure the captain is ready to see you."

A few soldiers, some in only half uniform, leaned against the fence. One tipped his non-military broad-brimmed hat at Soonie, and the others just leered.

She moved closer to her uncle. "How many soldiers are here?"

Uncle Isak shrugged. "Ten or fifteen. Years ago, during the wars, fifty to a hundred soldiers would have lived here, but now most of the native people have been banished to reservations, there are no need for that many.

The men here now are mostly to keep an eye on the borders and make sure trappers and drifters behave themselves."

Soonie wiped her eyes, still watering from the dust, and shook out her skirt. She pulled her shawl a little tighter around her shoulders.

Uncle Isak found a bit of shade cast by a building and leaned against the wall, closing his blue eyes. His chin dipped down towards his chest before jerking up again.

Soonie's heart filled with tenderness. *He works so hard and cares so much for his people. Everyone in the settlement would be dead, in prison, or back on the reservation if it weren't for him and Brave Storm. And he's never asked for a thing in return, only the freedom to live as he wishes.*

Lieutenant Ford stuck his head out of the door. "Captain'll see you now." He swung the door open and they followed him inside.

A fresh coat of whitewash shone on the walls. Soonie was surprised to see a large painting, depicting a ship at sea, hanging at the back of the room. A desk sat below it, wood shavings dusting the top of the otherwise tidy surface.

A man entered the room, so tall he had to stoop to pass through the frame.

"Mr. Isak, good to see you." A broad smile revealed a gap in his two front teeth. Powder blue eyes twinkled under bushy eyebrows, and his mustache looked like a thin gray scrub-brush. He held out a leathered hand. "Miss Susannah Ekhart, I presume? I expected an old maid, and who comes in? Why, the purtiest girl I've seen in these parts!"

Why do men always say the rudest things and believe them to be compliments? Soonie studied his face. The man was completely oblivious. She took the offered hand and gingerly shook it. "A pleasure," she said, through a forced smile.

Captain Wilkerson gestured to two rough wooden chairs across from the desk. He waited for Soonie and Isak to sit, then settled down behind the desk.

"What can I do for you today?"

Soonie glanced at Uncle Isak, who raised his eyebrows and nodded.

"Sir, as you know, I came here to teach the children of the settlement."

"Hmmm-Hmmm." The captain frowned. He pulled a Bowie knife from a drawer in the desk and began to whittle a stick. Shavings curled into the pile like twisting vines. "Commendable effort, showing the children how to be useful in society."

Soonie's cheeks burned and she choked back the retort buzzing through her brain. *Where do people get this idea we should 'usher the children into civilization' by 'making them useful'? Why don't we educate them for their own sakes, so they can become the people God created them to be in the first place?*

Instead of these words she said, "Our educational supplies are extremely limited. I realize books would be too much to ask for, but perhaps you could help us procure some slates?"

Captain Wilkerson stroked his beard. "Slates, you say? Oh yes, had those when I was a boy. Chalk and whatnot. Dangerous to acquire. Very dangerous indeed. Why would we ask for slates here, in the fort? No one

77

questions extra clothing, food or blankets. Even some farming equipment can slide by without a problem."

The shavings continued to snake into the pile. So many moments of silence ticked by that Soonie began to wonder if the captain had forgotten they were sitting there.

Finally, Uncle Isak leaned forward, resting his chin on steepled fingers. He cleared his throat.

A fly buzzed around the room, landing on the captain's knife hilt. He blew it off and glanced up. "I have a plan."

Soonie let out her caught breath and shifted in her seat. Sweat slid down her calves, pooling into her moccasin boots.

"In a few weeks, a couple of my men will be going to the nearest town to order supplies from a shopkeeper there. I doubt he'll have the slates in stock, and it might take a month or two for him to get them, but he's a greedy man, and not likely to ask questions."

Soonie jiggled her leg slightly, hoping the movement might send a bit of cool air beneath her chair. "And you don't think the order will be a risk to the settlement?"

The captain put down his knife and ran a finger over the freshly smoothed wood. "Miss Eckhart, every letter that comes through here, every padded food shipment, every extra supply is a risk for your settlement. Your uncle here and the other leaders know it."

Uncle Isak nodded. "But Soonie believes the slates are needed for the children's education, and we trust her judgment."

A weight settled over Soonie's shoulders like none ever placed there before. *Are the slates important enough to risk everyone's freedom? Are my letters from home so vital? How very ignorant I have been. But no, we need the slates. I've thought it over so many times, and I can't think of another option.*

With a sorrowful look at his stick the captain put it down, wiped his hands on a cloth and rose.

Soonie and Isak followed suit.

"Thank you both for coming," Captain Wilkerson said. "Isak, always nice to have you visit."

He nodded to Soonie. "I hope our paths will cross another day, Miss Eckhart."

"Thank you for your time." Isak reached into the pouch slung from his waist. "We have items for trade, of course." He placed a handful of beaded bracelets on the desk's one clean area.

The captain's eyes lit up. "These are perfect. Isak, you never disappoint."

Isak nodded and turned to go.

"Oh, I wanted to mention," Captain Wilkerson spoke as Isak and Soonie reached the door. "My men have encountered a group of drifters recently. Shifty fellows. Maybe trappers. My soldiers warned them about the 'haunted hills,' but we can't keep them from wandering around if they decide to explore. Wanted to make sure you knew."

Uncle Isak pursed his lips. "Thank you."

Lieutenant Ford waited for them outside the door. He escorted them past the surly guard and back to their horses.

On the way home, Soonie contemplated the precarious situation the settlement people were in. *I must remember, every day, to place my life in the hands of my Father. It's the only place where anyone can truly be safe.*

9

Onions and Hides

After they returned to the settlement and cared for the horses, Uncle Isak led Soonie to Brave Storm's tipi. "We'll stop by and tell him about the slates."

He called through the tent flap. "Brave Storm, *maruawe*! Are you there?"

"*Haw*," came a muffled reply. "Come in."

Uncle Isak lifted the flap and gestured for Soonie to step inside.

Soonie paused to study the scenes of wars and achievements painted on the outside of the tent. She'd only spoken to the camp's other leader once, and he'd barely glanced her way, only answering questions indirectly to Uncle Isak. Brave Storm seemed to prefer keeping to himself. She hadn't seen him at any of the settlement's events.

She took a hesitant step through the flap. The area inside the tipi was larger than one would think from seeing the outside, about twelve feet across the middle. The scent of sweat and animal hides thickened the air.

Because winter had not yet come, cooking was done outside. Most of the space was devoted to sleeping and storage. Clay pots, baskets and clothing were stacked neatly by the walls. An array of knives, spears and bows hung from the support posts.

Brave Storm sat in the corner, with a hunk of cornbread in his hand. No feathers adorned his graying braids, and a simple yellow streak ran along his cheekbones. His shoulders were thrown back, and anyone could tell by the way he carried himself that he was a man who commanded respect. "Isak, how goes the day?" he asked.

Soonie shrank back against the tipi's side. She wasn't afraid of the Kiowa leader, but she had no wish to be in a place where she didn't belong.

"We have returned from the fort," said Uncle Isak. "Captain Wilkerson said he could arrange for the slates."

The older man grunted. "He is a good man to provide such things for our children."

Uncle Isak dipped his head. "Yes. But he gave other news. A group of drifters happened by the fort a few days ago. Captain Wilkerson said they might be trappers, and we should keep watch in case they come too close."

Brave Storm scowled. Putting down his food, he rose to his feet and went to the sleeping area. He kicked at a large pile of blankets.

The covers moved, and Lone Warrior sat up, blinking. "Wh-what?" His eyes widened when he saw Soonie.

Soonie gripped a support pole to keep from stumbling back. She turned her head and bit her lip, suppressing a giggle. He looked just like a baby owl, wakened in the daytime.

"Isak tells me there are strangers in the area. How did you not know this? You must keep better watch." Brave Storm clenched his fists.

Lone Warrior's back stiffened. He pressed folded arms against his bare chest. "Father, we saw these men days ago, two miles away. They wouldn't know day from night-time, and a child could see their trail from the hilltop. We are in no danger from them."

"Still, you did not tell me." Brave Storm hissed. Soonie almost expected to see flashes of lightning shoot from his eyes.

Lone Warrior stood and stretched. He wore buckskin trousers and nothing else. He grabbed an onion from a basket and took a bite from the raw vegetable, the pungent smell permeating the tent. "They posed no threat," he said between bites. "I did not wish to trouble you with news of vermin."

Soonie glanced from the tipi's flap to Uncle Isak's face. *Should I leave?* Comanche and Kiowa men did not often discuss important matters in front of women. It seemed as though, caught up in this argument, they had forgotten she was there.

I should have gone straight home.

Lone Warrior did not have his porcupine cap on today. His hair was sleek and black, parted in the middle and gathered into two thin braids. His shoulders were wide, brown as oak leaves in the winter.

I wish he would put on a shirt. Even though many of the settlement's men walked around bare-chested, Soonie still felt uncomfortable seeing people traipse around in almost no clothes.

Lone Warrior caught Soonie's eye. His mouth quirked up at the corners.

Brave Storm kneeled down and poked at the fire with a stick. "You must stay close, my son. There's no reason for those men to be in this place unless they are coming for something valuable. We aren't the only ones who know the muskrat and beaver are plentiful here, and people in the city pay a great deal of money for pelts. If someone found us, they could turn our people in for a reward and take what little we own. Men like that live only to steal and destroy."

Lone Warrior threw his onion peel into the fire. "We are Kiowa. We do not skulk like coyotes in the grass. Those men should not hunt for trouble. They might find it."

These last words were delivered in a low, dangerous tone that sent a shiver down Soonie's spine. *Does he not care about the safety of the children? His own brother could be at risk. A few drifters may not pose much of a threat, but what if they brought in a posse?* Soonie tightened her lips, knowing her thoughts would not be welcomed or heeded.

Brave Storm rose and stepped over to his son, leaning close until their foreheads almost touched. "We have had this talk. I fought the last wars against the white man, when your feet did not yet have the strength to move you across the earth. Hundreds of men, women and children fell around me. I slipped on their blood as I ran away. If we wish to have freedom, we will lay low."

"How can that be freedom?" Lone Warrior snorted. His eye caught Soonie's once more. "And why has this white woman," he spat the words, "been allowed in to listen to our talks? I still think she is a spy, sent to find our weaknesses."

"That's ridiculous!" Soonie could hold her tongue no longer. "I'm here to help the children of my people. I did not choose my heritage, but I am proud of both sides."

Uncle Isak wiped his forehead. "Soonie . . .'

She turned to face Brave Storm. "I realize the heart of a woman holds little value in this place, but I promise mine beats strong and true. I would never betray you."

Brave Storm rubbed his chin. "I do not fear the white blood in your veins. I am not afraid of Isak or those in this camp with white ancestors. I am more worried about young men who travel the countryside with no care for what happens to anyone else."

Lone Warrior's face grew dark, and his fingers twitched over his knife-hilt. "I only go out for the hunt, to keep watch, and to pray. The game is scarce, with the fort nearby. The town to the north continues to expand its hunting territory. I've had to travel further to get enough food for everyone."

Isak bowed his head. "We will have to manage with what game we can find nearby, the stores of canned and dried food, and our fall gardens. At least until the winter snows drive these men to the warmth of their towns. Until we know they are gone for sure, everyone must stay close to the settlement, for the safety of all."

The younger man uttered a Kiowa word Soonie was sure wasn't polite. He pulled up the tent flap, gave her one more withering look, and ducked out.

"I'm going home. Good night, Uncle Isak. Brave Storm." Soonie gave a tiny curtsey and left the tent.

###

When Soonie walked into the door of Grandmother Eagle's home, she found Molly working at the small table. Pungent and spicy scents wafted from an array of herbs and plants spread out before her.

"Hello! I was wondering when you would return." Molly gave Soonie a hug and went back to sorting through the piles.

"What is all this?" Soonie picked up a bunch of dried yellow flowers and sniffed at them. A cloud of pollen puffed out from the petals and made her sneeze.

"You have a yellow nose," Molly giggled. "Here, let me help you." She dusted the powder off Soonie's face with the corner of her shawl.

"Sorry." Soonie put the flowers back.

"I'm looking through Grandmother's herbs. The cold season always brings sickness and ailments. I want to be sure we have enough supplies to make medicines. Though many of Grandmother Eagle's remedies are based on her understanding of spirits, some of these herbs are also used for physical healing."

Soonie nodded. "I recognize some of the plants my grandmother gathered. She always helped people in town when they got sick, at least, before the doctor came. People still ask her for advice sometimes, when they can't afford the doctor. Some folks come for prayer as much as anything. Grandma Louise prays for everyone who walks through the door."

Molly set a basket on the table and packed some of the bags and containers into it. "Isn't it interesting, how our grandmothers are so alike, yet so different?"

Soonie pictured the two elderly women together, one thin and wizened, one plump and pink. Both possessed such wisdom. "I almost think they might be friends."

"Perhaps." Molly finished clearing the table and tapped a finger against her lips. "I'm going to have to gather more plants before the first frost. We go through so many tinctures and some will be gone soon."

"Are the plants far away? Because Captain Wilkerson said a group of strange men have been wandering around the hills. Lone Warrior saw them too. Brave Storm said he wants everyone to stay close to the settlement for a while, until the men are gone."

Molly ran a cornhusk broom over the table, the dried husks making 'scritch-scratch' noises over the surface. "Grandmother Eagle will speak to him. She has the final say in camp, did you know that? The eagle doctor is respected above all others, male or female. I will be allowed to gather these plants, for the health of our people."

"Then I will come along," Soonie decided. "I used to gather herbs with my grandma, so I know some of the plants to look for. We won't have school this week, the children are taking a break to help with winter preparations."

"We'll have to go to the eastern hills." Molly hung the broom at its place beside the wash basin. "The terrain is too rough for horses and it takes two or three hours to walk there."

"Wylder and I used to go for day-long rambles in the woods all the time," Soonie replied.

"It's settled," said Molly. "Tomorrow is Sunday, so we will go on Monday."

Soonie filled a pot with water and placed it on top of the ancient stove. *A day to spend in the woods with my friend.* She would have danced around the room if not for the danger of hitting the wall and bringing the whole home down around their ears. She could hardly wait.

10
Gathering

An autumn sun rose over the trees, stretching out colorful rays in praise to the sky. Cool air whispered over Soonie's face, as though apologizing for the past misery of summer.

Molly climbed the hill like a squirrel, without missing a step.

A little spring bubbled from a crack in the side of the hill and flowed through a miniature forest of springy ferns. All types of flora grew in the fertile soil, soaked in the minerals the spring produced.

Grandmother Eagle had not bothered to ask permission of the settlement's leaders. When Molly mentioned Brave Storm's decree, she had snorted.

"I will pray to the eagle spirits. They will protect you," she had said, waving them out the door.

I'm glad I put my faith in the Almighty and not a bird. Soonie squinted up at the azure sky, filled with feathery clouds. She hadn't even seen an eagle since she arrived at the settlement, only a few red-tailed hawks and dozens of buzzards. *And we don't really want any help from them.*

A patch of wood sorrel grew near the path and she bent down to gather a handful. The clover-shaped leaves had a mild sour flavor, similar to a lemon, that would go well with their lunch of dried meat.

Molly pointed up the ridge. "The day is passing quickly, and I would like to get to the top of this hill before noon. I've come to this place often, and some of our most needed herbs grow up there." She continued up the ridge.

Soonie studied the quiver slung across Molly's thin shoulders as she followed. The long bag was made of hide and decorated with porcupine quills that were cut into small segments and sewn in rows. The edge was trimmed with elk teeth, which Soonie had learned were particularly rare.

"Wylder and I made bows and arrows when we were children," Soonie said. "But my quiver wasn't nearly as fancy as yours."

"The bow and quiver belonged to my father. And this arrow was his as well." Molly pulled out the longest arrow, which was tipped with an obsidian arrowhead. "It also belonged to my grandfather. No matter how many times they used it in the hunt, it was never broken, and they always found it again."

Soonie traced the chipped surface of the gleaming stone. "It's beautiful."

Placing the arrow back into the quiver, Molly began to climb again, speaking over her shoulder. "For a very long time, Comanche women were not allowed to carry weapons, but here the danger is too great to go without some way to defend ourselves. So the custom has changed."

Soonie touched the hilt of her own knife. "Seems like a silly rule. I'm glad it's different now."

Molly turned. "Yes, many changes have come to pass, and more will follow. Women of most places have rules holding them back, don't they?"

"Yes." Soonie considered the few wealthy women she knew. Ladies who chose to parade around in ribcage-crushing corsets and hats so large they could barely move their necks for fear the headwear would plummet to the ground. Women who spent their days picking out garbled tunes on a piano or doing needlepoint. "I believe some of the boundaries have been built with our own hands."

The girls stopped often to gather berries, stems and leaves. On occasion, Molly used a sharp stone to dig for roots. They stored all these plants in pouches, slung around their hips. Further up the ridge they traveled, crumbles of dirt sliding down in steady streams beneath their feet.

Long past noon, the two girls had gathered all they could carry. Almost at the top of the bluff, they stopped for a lunch of bread and dried meat, along with Soonie's sorrel.

Molly patted a bulging sack. "Grandmother Eagle will be pleased. We've had better luck than usual this year, probably because of the rains."

Soonie leaned back against a tree and closed her eyes. Her thoughts wandered, as they usually did, hundreds of miles to home. *I wonder what Zillia is doing?* One letter had arrived from her friend, with the assurance that all was well with the baby. Zillia was several months along now. Soonie pictured her, round with child and glowing with happiness. The doctor had confirmed Zillia's guess; the baby would arrive sometime in February.

Soonie nibbled on a pink sorrel blossom. Pink . . . surely the baby would be a girl. After all the shenanigans Orrie had put his sister through, it seemed only fair.

"Have you ever helped deliver a baby?" she asked Molly.

"No." Molly tipped her head to the side. "Grandmother Eagle will not allow me to attend births. A woman who is to become an eagle doctor, like I was supposed to, cannot assist in such matters until she has been married a long time and her children have grown. But birth is a sacred, happy time for our people. I have a book with some information and I'll have to learn about it if I am to be a doctor someday.

"When my cousin came to see us last year, he told us about a woman doctor who had come to the reservation. She received a certificate from a university. If she was able to do so, perhaps I could as well."

Soonie clasped her hands together. "Oh, Molly, how wonderful. Imagine how much you would learn."

Molly's smile faded into a worried frown. "But perhaps a Comanche girl would not be allowed to study with white people. I do not know."

"Maybe we could write this woman a letter and see what she thinks."

"Perhaps." Molly stared at the ground, a wistful smile tugging at her lips.

A slight movement rippled through the brush.

In a flash, Molly was on her feet, her bow drawn and an arrow on the string. "Show yourself," she called.

Hairs stood up on the back of Soonie's neck. Her eyes sought Molly's for some explanation.

The girl stared past her.

Should I get to my feet? Duck down? Run?

Molly's eyes widened.

Rough hands grabbed Soonie's hair and snapped her head back. A sharp object brushed her throat.

"I suggest you put the bow down, Missy," a voice rasped in Soonie's ear.

No, no. Not here. Not today. We are so far from help.

Molly lowered the bow. Two men came behind her, each grabbing an elbow. She struggled for only an instant before she grew still, her heaving chest the only movement.

Soonie's neck stung as the object pressed harder against her skin. Warnings darted from Molly's eyes, and she held back all but the tiniest breaths.

A fourth man stepped in between the girls and their captors. He removed his hat, revealing a bush of white hair. "Well, well, well, men. I guess there's more to hunt in these hills than beavers and fox."

I've seen this man before. Soonie searched through her memories to a time when her heart beat almost as fast. *That day on the road, when we were traveling to the settlement.*

The three men in her line of vision were unkempt and unwashed. Their clothing was dirty and ragged.

Soonie closed her eyes. *God, please, please,* were all the words she could think to pray. She scanned the area as far as her eyes could move without turning her head. *Anything. Anywhere.*

A jagged fingernail poked her cheek. The man in front of her bent close and opened a mouth full of rotted, broken teeth. "You girls live close by? Or did the birds drop you off as a little present for us hard-workin' trappers?"

He nodded to her invisible captor, and she felt the blade leave her skin.

Molly's eyes had closed, and her lips moved with no sound. Soonie knew she was praying too.

"Yup, you girls are purty nice, for injun girls." The white-haired man grasped Soonie's chin between his thumb and forefinger and stared into her face. "You almost look white. I figger you must be a half-breed. So I'd bet you know a bit of English, at least. We've been through that town east of here, and we know they don't allow your kind 'round these parts. So I'm gonna ask you one more time, and you'd better answer me." He took the knife from the man who held her and shoved it close to her nose. "Where did you come from?"

Suddenly, Molly swung her elbows up to smash the faces of both her abductors. They staggered back. She lowered her head and barreled into one man's gut, sending him sprawling to the ground.

The white-haired man turned. Soonie kicked at the knife, causing the blade to slice the side of his face. She wrenched her arms free, pulled out her own blade and whirled to face her surprised captor, a thin man with no beard.

He jumped back in time to avoid having his belly cut open. "Hal, she's a wild cat!" he yelled.

If I can just get past him, to the right--.

A jolt of pain ran through Soonie's arm as another man twisted it behind her. He shoved her, and she landed hard on the rocks. Her lungs pressed against her ribcage, begging for air to fill them again.

Molly screamed, and the men cursed.

I need to take a breath. I have to get up.

She rolled on her back, and a heavy body thudded to the ground beside her, an arm flinging over her stomach. The young man's glassy eyes stared into hers. His hairless chin was slack, and an arrow stuck out of his chest.

A blanket of silence fell over the ridge.

Soonie pushed the man's arm away and scooted back to avoid the blood spilling over his side. Her arm ached and a new pain darted up her ankle when she tried to put weight on it.

A different man stood by the undergrowth, watching the trappers as they fled. Soonie could still hear cursing and crashing, but it got further and further away.

The man wore buckskin clothing, and his brown arms gleamed with sweat and oil.

"Lone Warrior, how..." she tried to stand, but her ankle gave way beneath her and she sat down again. "Ouch!"

Molly flew to her side, a scarlet handprint from a slap glowing on her face. "Oh, Soonie, are you all right? I thought you might have been knocked out when you fell."

Lone Warrior came to kneel beside her. He rubbed his neck and his lips twisted into a frown. "I sent Thomas and Gray Fox after those men. Better if they don't make it out alive, but they have horses and we did not bring our animals. We were hunting in the gully when we saw their camp and decided to see what they were doing here."

He touched Soonie's ankle, and she trembled as he probed her foot with gentle fingers. "Do you think it might be broken?"

Molly pushed his hand out of the way. "I'll be the judge of that. Clumsy man." She tugged at Soonie's moccasin strings.

Soonie bit her lip to hold back a gasp, but tears flowed down her cheeks.

"You are causing her pain," Lone Warrior said sharply.

"I need to find out what's wrong." Molly pulled at the leather. "I'm going to have to cut the straps, but I'll fix them later. The ankle is already so swollen."

"Do what you need to do," Soonie said, through gritted teeth.

Molly drew out her knife and snapped through the supple leather. She eased the shoe off the foot. "It doesn't look broken. But if touch causes this much pain, you will not be able to walk home."

A strong sapling stretched over Soonie's spot on the ground, and she grasped the trunk and tried to pull herself to her feet. The pain enveloped her entire being and spots danced before her eyes. She sat back down. "I'm putting us all in danger," she murmured. "Those men could return at any moment."

Lone Wolf stood and stared into the brush. "I don't believe they will come back today. Only three remained in the group, two were bleeding."

Soonie's eyes rested on the dead man, whom she had somehow forgotten in the last few moments. "What about him? Do we know who he was?"

"A man who made a bad choice," said Molly.

Lone Warrior nudged the body with his foot. "The others will want revenge for their friend," he said softly. "But not tonight."

11
Firelight

Thomas and Gray Fox returned within an hour.

"The men escaped." Gray Fox swiped a hand across his brow. "God only knows how those horses made it down the ridge."

Lone Warrior turned away and kicked a large, rotten tree stump down the hill. He snapped around. "It is as I feared. Let's get rid of this *tdahle* and then we'll decide what to do."

"What's a *tdahle*?" Soonie whispered to Molly as Thomas and Gray Fox picked up the dead body. Lone Warrior followed them down the ridge.

"A rat," replied Molly. "How does your ankle feel?"

"Still throbbing." Soonie stretched out her leg and tried not to think about the pain. She was almost grateful for her injury so she wouldn't have to watch as the trapper disappeared beneath the soft earth.

After a time, Lone Warrior came back alone. "I sent Thomas and Gray Fox to the settlement to fetch my

Cactus Pear. She's the most sure-footed of our horses. They will not be able to make the trip back until the morning. Even the best horse in the world couldn't get through that ravine at night. I will stay here and keep you safe."

"I—I can try to walk." Soonie tried to speak with confidence.

"No, you won't." Molly spread the girls' shawls over a patch of ferns. "And though we are strong, we can't carry you all that way on a stretcher. Staying the night is a good plan." She placed the packs on one end of the makeshift bed. "These will work for pillows. We'll be snug as rabbits."

Lone Warrior began to gather small sticks. He piled them beneath the rocky overhang.

Soonie found it difficult to pull her eyes away. Thick veins stood out in his hands when he grasped each twig, but every placement was gentle, and deliberate, as though he was creating a work of art.

He glanced up. "How is your foot?"

"I'll be all right."

He made a small noise in his throat and went back to work. "I'm building the fire here, so the smoke will filter through these rocks. Less chance of being seen."

"Why build a fire at all? We have already eaten." ·

Lone Warrior chuckled. "Yes, but the wolves have not." He gave her a tiny smile.

A kind look for me? A tingling Soonie had never felt before surged through her whole self.

Dusk settled in a cloudy haze, covering all but a few hopeful stars. No moon rose to bid good evening to the campers on the hill.

Soonie sank back with a sigh, resting the injured foot on one of the satchels. "I haven't felt this useless since I was seven and caught the measles. Grandma kept finding me out of bed, trying to drag myself around the house to do chores. Weeks passed before I felt better." She groaned. "I hope I recover faster this time. I have so many plans for school next week."

Using a rock, Molly ground a handful of berries to a pulp and scooped them into a leaf. She gave the makeshift plate to Soonie. "This should at least dull the ache."

Soonie took an experimental taste and made a face. *The pain might be better.*

Molly watched her closely until she swallowed the rest. The bitterness lingered inside her mouth.

Lone Warrior nodded to the sleeping area. "You both should try to get some rest."

Molly didn't protest. She curled up in her shawl and within minutes, fell asleep.

Every time Soonie closed her eyes, the face of the young trapper floated before them. One moment, his soul had been inside his body, wherever souls reside. The next instant, gone. No chance to change his mind, no opportunity to ask for redemption.

She sat up and scooted over to the fire. Bark popped in the flames and sent sparks floating to the heavens. *Do our souls look like that when we die? Some bright and happy, eager to meet their Creator, and others dark and cold, knowing the gates of Hell await?*

Lone Warrior turned from the ledge where he was keeping watch. "He made his choice," he said.

Soonie gave a short, surprised laugh. "Was my distress that obvious?"

"Out here, we see much of death. Sometimes we have to kill. Every man chooses their own path. You and Molly fought like warriors today."

Soonie rested her chin on folded hands. "Narrow is the road that leads to righteousness, and wide is the path that leads to destruction."

"At the reservation's school, I studied the Bible's scriptures. I believe in God. But what good are the white man's words when he acts differently?" Lone Warrior's eyes flashed in the firelight. "The white man quotes the Bible verse, 'Thou Shalt not kill.' Yet if I had not killed today, you and Molly would be dead."

Soonie shuddered. *Does he always have to be so direct?* "I believe men should be judged by their own merits. Not all white men are the same. Not all Comanche and Kiowa men have the same hearts. We should live under our own names, and let God be our judge."

"I hear the voice of God," said Lone Warrior. "In the sacred lodge, with Peyote."

Peyote? Soonie had only heard the drug referenced a few times. Uncle Isak had told her Peyote was a cactus. Swallowing the plant would cause hallucinations and visions. *Would God use such a substance to communicate with His people?* She shook her head. God spoke to her often, sometimes out loud, and sometimes with a gentle nudge inside her heart. And all she'd had to do was be still and listen.

She looked Lone Warrior in the eye. "If you believe in God, why are you filled with so much anger?"

He stepped out of the circle of light and into the trees' shadows. His lithe, long shape straightened as he craned his neck to see over the rocks. "When I lived on the reservation, all the children were friends. We played games and sang songs. We taught each other our sacred dances, both Comanche and Kiowa. Even though white men gave us far less than the promised food and supplies, and we often felt the pinch of hunger, laughter and friendship helped to warm our days and fill our bellies.

"At seventeen, I left children's games behind. Quanah Parker, the chief at Fort Sill, put me in charge of feeding the cattle.

"I'd just returned from my work for the noon meal when I heard a clatter from the road. Three shiny carts, drawn by the most beautiful horses I'd ever seen, came around the bend.

"A man in a black coat came out of first one and told the adults he would take children aged ten to fifteen to the train station. They would have to attend a school far away, to learn to be useful citizens.

"The people in the carriages made the children change into white men's clothes. They would not let them take anything from the reservation. Not dolls, not weapons. Nothing." Lone Warrior closed his eyes and rubbed his forehead. "I'll never forget as I watched the first group climb into the carts. Some looked excited. A few of the youngest cried. Mothers stood outside with helpless hands.

"Chief Quanah said it was for the best. He'd seen his people almost wiped out by starvation and sickness, and he felt that learning trades and receiving an education was a good thing for the children. But my father held Timothy close to his side.

"Isak spread the word of a military post, several hours to the south, led by a captain who owed him his life. We didn't want our fate in the hands of yet another white man, but Isak pleaded with us.

"Isak's sister, Roberta, clutched the hands of her two little sons. She was convinced the men would be back for all the children, even the babies.

"In the hours before the buggies were to come for more passengers, our families packed what they could."

"After being on the reservation so long?" Soonie couldn't imagine. "How did you all get away?"

"Quanah saw the tears of the women, and he waved us on. Thirty people left that day, with only the items our horses could carry. Much later, he sent two wagons, filled with some supplies. I don't know what he told the soldiers who kept watch over the reservation. But Quanah was a rich man. He must have used bribes."

"And the children who were taken? Did their parents ever hear from them?"

A tear gleamed in the corner of Lone Warrior's eye, and trickled through his face paint, down to his chin. "From what we heard, no one ever saw them again. I assume they were taught to despise the Comanche heritage." His face twisted, as though he fought to hold in further, bitter words.

Soonie twisted her hands under her shawl. "Uncle Isak brought my cousins to my grandparents four years ago. He said there had been many sicknesses." She remembered the first day she had seen little Henry and Will, with their thin, pinched faces. *Would they have survived at the settlement?*

"Isak's sister died of a fever that spread through camp right after we moved in. Many children were orphaned during that time."

"So you escaped one tragedy, only to fall into another." Soonie murmured.

"Yes." Lone Warrior stared into the fading embers. "But we have found better ways to grow food. We are less hungry than we were on the reservation, when the government was to help us. And we are free. It was worth the price."

Soonie stretched out trembling fingers and touched Lone Warrior's hand. "I'm sorry for all the hardships you have been through. It must have been terrible."

The young man's eyebrows traveled up to his porcupine quills and his lips twitched. He said nothing, only stared at her small hand covering his dark one. For a long time, they stayed that way, watching the fire burn down to darkened coals.

12

Tipi Talk

Soonie limped up to Uncle Isak's tipi, leaning heavily on the walking stick Hershel and Felix had presented to her that morning. Seven days had passed since the injury. Molly had decided she had just pulled a few muscles, and said it would heal before too long. The pain had dwindled, but she still couldn't rest all her weight on the foot.

Uncle Isak sewed a tear that ran up the side of the tent. Leathered fingers tugged a large, bone needle through the material with practiced technique.

He turned to Soonie. "How did school go today?"

"Pretty well." Soonie picked up a second needle and poked holes along the sides of another tear. "Mira can read short words now, and Little Boar has finally learned how to write his name. Even the older boys have been on their best behavior since I hurt my ankle. Suppose I've garnered their sympathy."

Uncle Isak nodded, intent on his work. Sweat stained his shirt where his heavy braids hung against the fabric. No one in the settlement was fooled by the warm air that had blown through earlier in the week. Each member worked to weatherize the shelters with what materials they had available.

At first, Soonie had been excited by the prospect of snow. Winter storms in Bastrop seldom brought more than a flurry. But when she considered the tipis and hastily-built shanties the people called their homes, she couldn't believe they had already lasted through four winters in this place. She learned that during the coldest days, the people crowded into as few homes as possible, sharing fuel, food and body heat.

Tipis were not meant to stay in one place for a long time. In times before the reservation, the cone-shaped structures had been packed up and moved when a group traveled. Soonie's mother had said when she was a little girl, she'd helped the older women take down these portable homes. The skins, stiff from the elements, were removed from the poles, then beaten with sticks to make them supple enough to roll into impossibly tight bundles. The tall, straight sticks were pulled down and tied together with leather strips. The whole thing would be done in minutes.

Molly had told Soonie the settlement's members would have all preferred to live in tipis, but hides needed to create and repair them had become scarce. Deer and elk were rarely found in these hills, and buffalo had been gone for decades. Pelts from rabbits and the other small game found in the area could not be used for construction. A shame, for the Kiowa families owned tipis that had been passed on through generations, and paintings depicting decades of hunts and battles faded a little more with every season.

Some of the tipis had been repaired so many times, with various hides, blankets and cloths, that beneath the layers of dust they looked like patchwork quilts. Each piece of material added on had to be shaped carefully as to not waste any of the fabric, and then rubbed with tallow or animal fat to make it waterproof.

"Any word on the slates?" Soonie asked. Uncle Isak had just returned from the fort.

"Yes." Uncle Isak's face brightened. "Captain Wilkerson said he could get eight, and that they would be here soon. And another good thing. He said nothing about the man Lone Warrior killed, so he did not know about it. Lone Warrior was right. Those men were trying to hide something. A good trapping line, perhaps. I've heard people in the east are paying a lot of money for beaver pelts to make hats."

Soonie stared at him. "You didn't tell the captain what happened?"

A muscle in Uncle Isak's cheek twitched. "Soonie, I trust the man with my life, but it is good to know when not to speak. Why stir up trouble? Lone Warrior will tell me if he and his friends see anything suspicious."

Soonie remembered the look on Lone Warrior's face after the young man had been shot. *Or he'll take care of the problem himself.*

"I'm surprised they wouldn't try to avenge their friend's death. Those men were evil. If Lone Warrior, Thomas and Gray Fox hadn't come along, they would have done something terrible to Molly and me." Soonie shuddered. She ripped a piece of cloth from an old blanket and held it up against a hole.

"I don't think we'll see them again." Uncle Isak stabbed his needle into another section of hide. "Even if they found this place, three men couldn't fight all of us. They would have to notify the law. A week has passed. If they didn't have something to hide they'd have already been out here looking for us, with help."

Soonie sat back against a tree to rest her leg. "I hope you're right. I don't ever want to see Hal and his friends again."

Lone Warrior had been gone most of the time since that night at the fire. If he wasn't hunting, he was out on watch. The few times Soonie had passed him, he merely asked about her ankle, nodded when she answered, and moved on. She decided the instance at the campfire had been merely a sympathetic interlude and nothing more. *Why am I even dwelling on it? Why do I give that man a second thought?*

These thoughts brought another part of the campfire conversation to Soonie's mind. "Uncle Isak, Lone Warrior told me about an unsettling practice he and his friends are involved in. I'm worried mostly for the younger boys."

Uncle Isak's shoulders sagged. "The Peyote."

"Yes. I'm surprised you and Brave Storm allow them to partake of such a thing."

Uncle Isak tied off his line of stitches. "Soonie, don't forget. You are new to this place. Our people do many things you cannot understand."

Though the words were delivered gently, they still stung. Soonie brushed away a sudden tear. *Will I ever understand?*

Uncle Isak glanced up, and his eyes filled with compassion. "Ah, Soonie. I know you care for the children's safety. As far as I've seen, the only ill effects from Peyote have been dreams and deep sleep. Because of my Christian faith, I do not use Peyote, though some Christ-followers think the plant helps them hear from God. Lone Warrior and his friends believe this way. They have built a Peyote lodge. It's quite a distance from camp and the younger boys are not allowed to go there. We can say what happens here at the settlement, but we cannot make the choice for them."

Soonie's shoulders sagged. Of course Uncle Isak would leave it up to the young men to decide.

Her foot throbbed, and she reached down to rub it. The memory of another touch caused her heart to jump.

Lone Warrior. She'd never dreamed coming to this place would lead to such scrambled feelings. Those deep brown eyes held so much wisdom. He was a man of integrity, who loved his people. And he had saved her life. *But he would have done the same for anyone.*

If only Zillia were here! Molly was a good friend, but not close enough to discuss such complicated issues. She frowned. No, such thoughts shouldn't be shared with anyone. She and the young Kiowa man were so different. He held an obvious contempt for her white lineage.

"As though I can help it."

"What was that?" Uncle Isak peeked over the side of the tipi.

Soonie put up hands to cover her glowing cheeks. "Nothing, just thinking out loud."

Uncle Isak gathered his tools and stepped back to survey his work. "Hopefully, that'll hold for another winter. If not, you ladies might have to make room for me on the kitchen floor."

Soonie pulled herself up on her stick. "I suppose some things must be left in God's hands."

"Thank you for your help."

"Wish I could have done more," Soonie replied.

Uncle Isak rested his hand on her shoulder. "You have done more than you think, Little One. You are a strong and courageous woman, and I'm glad you have come. Go and rest, so you can be ready for what comes tomorrow."

Soonie stumped along the path with her makeshift cane. The tipi was situated within a crease in the rock, and as she came around the side, she heard men's loud voices.

Lone Warrior, Thomas and Gray Fox stumbled toward the center of the settlement, laughing and shoving each other.

"How is your foot?" asked Lone Warrior. His eyes rested on her for a moment, and then rolled to the side. He squinted and shook his head, then trained his focus on her again. This seemed to take a lot of effort.

"It's better, thank you." She lifted her chin and tried to pretend she didn't notice his condition. "I still have to use my stick, as you can see, but probably not much longer. And how are you? You look a little . . . poorly."

Lone Warrior flung his arms out to his friends. "We're all fine. Aren't we?"

Guffaws and loud agreements met his words.

"I'm glad to hear that." Soonie stood a little straighter. "I think you're all disgraceful. Everyone is working so hard and you—you're nothing but three lazy oafs."

Gray Fox stepped closer, until she could feel his hot breath on her cheeks. "We were out all night in the hills, watching for those men. So be careful about who you call lazy."

Lone Warrior pulled him back. "Don't pay any attention to her. She has no respect for us, or our ways." These last words ended in a hiss.

Accursed drug. Soonie pushed her way through the young men and prepared to scale the path to her house. Not an easy task with her crutch, but she would have crawled up on her knees before she asked one of them for help.

Halfway up the ridge, a twisted oak tree grew over the path, branches sprawled to the side. Partially uprooted during a flood long before, it had managed to hold on to the hillside and continue to grow in this unnatural fashion. Beneath the branches sat Timothy, eyes trained on Lone Warrior and his friends. When Soonie passed, he gazed up at her. "Isn't it wonderful?"

Soonie reached down and straightened one of the feathers in his hair. "What's wonderful?"

"They can go and speak to God, whenever they want!"

Soonie's ankle throbbed all the more from the walk up the hill, but she knelt beside the boy anyway. Dappled sunlight reached through the tree's branches and caught the sparkle of gypsum and quartz crystals in the rocks.

"Timothy, don't you remember what we talked about in school yesterday? We may pray to God whenever we wish. He is always listening."

The boy pulled a small knife from his belt and ran the edge along a tree branch. "But my brother says when he goes into the lodge, God talks back."

"I don't know if he really does hear God." Soonie frowned. "He's eating a plant that makes his thoughts scrambled. I don't believe God speaks to people that way."

"But what if it's true? What if you really could just eat a cactus to hear God? I've tried to talk to Him, many times, but I haven't heard anything. What if . . . what if I could hear my mother speak from Heaven?"

"Oh, Timothy." Soonie's heart melted, and she longed to reach out and comfort this motherless boy. But she knew the impulse would tear apart any bonds she had created with him, so she held back.

Timothy turned back to watch Lone Warrior and his group, staring after them until they disappeared below the ridge.

13
Dancing Night

Brother Jenkins sucked in his cheeks, which seemed paler than before, if that were possible. A few hairs sprouted over his chin, probably overlooked when shaving.

Soonie had missed attending church services. The weekly prayers and hymns shared in the school house by the settlement's believers were uplifting, but not the same to her as a sermon delivered by someone who studied and prepared for a journey into the Word.

But, like before, it seemed that every scripture Brother Jenkins chose, or at least his interpretation of them, steered the message in favor of the white man's superiority.

Most of the people in the Bible weren't even white. When Soonie was a little girl, Grandpa had told her that folks from the eastern lands, such as Hebrews, Greeks, Romans, and Syrians, were born with darker skin and eyes. What made white men so special? Her fingers tightened around her Bible. *How dare anyone say one race is superior to another? God created all men equal. How grieved He must be to hear teachers speak in His name and suggest such things.*

After the sermon, she pressed against the wall of the schoolhouse while everyone else rushed outside to prepare and partake of the meal served when the circuit preacher came.

Brother Jenkins paused and bowed to her on his way out. "Miss Eckhart, I'm glad to see you haven't given up the fight. How are things progressing?"

"My students are doing well." She decided not to add they'd probably taught her as much about Kiowa and Comanche culture as she had taught them about reading, writing and arithmetic.

He rubbed the missed hairs on his chin. "Good to hear, good to hear."

"Brother Jenkins, I would like to talk to you about your teaching."

Though he stared right at her, his eyes were vacant, like he didn't see her. He nodded. "Yes, yes, quite so." He fumbled in his pocket. "I'd almost forgotten. I have a letter for the girl you live with. Molly, I do believe? Can she even read?"

"You mean my second cousin? Of course she can read!" She snatched the letter from his hand. Beautiful script covered the front. "Oh, this is from the lady doctor at the reservation!"

Brother Jenkins bowed again. "Yes. She has expressed interest in meeting with Molly, I'm not sure why."

Soonie took a deep, steadying breath. "Because Molly would like to study medicine. She wrote to Doctor

Early a few weeks ago. We weren't sure if the letter would reach her."

Brother Jenkins straightened his jacket. "Doctor Early is a great help to the reservation, and when she asks for something, my fellowship generally tries to help. I will be in Dallas for a time, and then back through here in two weeks. If Molly is willing, I will accompany her to meet with the doctor in a town near the border, not far from Fort Sill. The doctor will be holding a clinic there on the tenth of November. Weather permitting, of course."

"Molly will be delighted." Soonie clutched the letter to her heart.

"I wished to see if you might come as well, Miss Eckhart. My fellowship would frown upon me traveling with a young lady and no chaperone. It would only be two days, so the children wouldn't miss too much school."

Could I handle being in this man's presence for two whole days? But Molly would want me along. Soonie nodded. "All right, Brother Jenkins, I will come." The angry words she had meant to say about the sermon slipped from her mind as she turned to leave.

Brother Jenkins touched her sleeve. "Will I see you again at lunch today?"

His face was so hopeful, Soonie almost felt sorry for him. All at once, it dawned on her. *This man believes he is doing right. God, please help him to understand the truth.*

She smiled as pleasantly as she could manage. "No, not today. Have a safe journey to Fort Sill."

She left him standing in the doorway, and felt his eyes follow her up the path to home.

###

"How will I ever wait two whole weeks!" Molly twirled in the sand, her shawl flapping like the wings of a hawk. "Think of it. I'll be able to meet Doctor Early, to discuss what I love with someone who has studied medicine in a real university. Brother Jenkins says she does all the doctoring for the reservation, and in many of the nearby towns as well."

"Mmm hmmm." Soonie had fallen so deep into her own thoughts she barely heard the younger girl's words. *Will Lone Warrior be at the gathering tonight? Does he even remember what happened last Monday? As if he'd care.* She kicked at a rock. At least she didn't have to walk with a stick anymore. Like Molly had predicted, her ankle was almost well.

I'm glad Brother Jenkins has already left for Fort Sill. I don't think I could handle both men in one place this evening.

The moon was halved in a clean line, as though a butcher had taken a cleaver to it with one, swift chop. Clouds rolled over it, and silver glinted around their edges.

A large fire danced in the center of camp. Everyone in the settlement had come, dressed in painted buckskins and elaborate shawls. A few of the women wore straw hats like those Soonie might see in a shop window back home, but these were trimmed Comanche style, with turkey feathers and porcupine quills.

Soonie leaned towards Molly. "I feel a bit underdressed."

"Don't be silly," said Molly. "Your mother's shawl is beautiful, and your hair looks lovely."

Soonie had followed Molly's lead and let her hair flow around her shoulders. She'd braided one tiny section and tied in a dove's feather.

Women stood in small groups chatting, while several of the Kiowa men sang and danced around the fire, stomping and shaking gourd rattles. A cluster of Comanche men standing to the side beat on small drums made of wood and skin.

The firelight cast a mesmerizing glow over the faces around it. The aroma of food swirled into the smoke, creating an otherworldly atmosphere.

Wildness stirred in Soonie's heart. *It's all so beautiful.*

The song was in Kiowa, but she had learned a few words since her arrival and phrases leapt out at her: a poem about hunting, horses, and bravery in the battle.

Lone Warrior stomped past her, wearing his father's buffalo robe. His eyes were closed, his head thrown back in song. Tonight, gold and green swirls covered his face instead of the angry black lines he usually sported. Soonie only recognized him because he was a head taller than the other men in the settlement. He looked happier than she had ever seen him.

She went to join Bright Flower, who was dishing out soup to hungry children.

"This is the first dance I've attended. At least, the first dance of the Comanche and Kiowa people."

"You have been to a white man's dance?" Laura stepped up to her, eyes shining. "Was it wonderful?"

"Not as wonderful as this." Soonie accepted the cup of soup Bright Flower handed her and ate a spoonful.

Rabbit. She allowed the rich, gamey taste to roll over her tongue before swallowing it down. The firelight poured into her eyes like molten gold and her body swayed to the driving beat, as though the drums and rattles were invisible puppeteer's hands bidding her to move.

Never before had she heard such music. Her mother had sung old Comanche songs, but one woman's chanting couldn't compare to this. The rhythm pounded through her being and spoke to her spirit as much as the words filling her ears.

She'd often made up dances when she was alone in the woods, for God. These had been inspired by the story of the prophetess Miriam dancing in the Bible. Tonight, so close to the stars, she felt a powerful connection to the spiritual realm.

The dance finished, and a group of women, including Tersa and Bright Flower, stepped forward. One picked up a rattle and swung it in graceful, rhythmic arcs while all the ladies sang the familiar, timeless words of the Doxology.

> *Praise God, from whom all blessings flow;*
> *Praise Him, all creatures here below;*

Soonie joined in, along with many others. They pressed in closer. Even those who were followers of the old ways put down their soup cups and paused in their conversation.

> *Praise Him above, ye heavenly host;*
> *Praise Father, Son, and Holy Ghost. Amen*

At the final 'Amen," a silence settled over the hillside.

A Presence trickled over Soonie like warm honey, filling her from the inside out. Love, so pure and strong she could hardly endure it, poured into her soul. She stumbled closer to the fire and fell on her knees, hands raised. *Oh thank you God. Thank you for the beauty of tonight. Thank you for all you have done for us. Thank you, thank you!*

After what seemed like a very long time, she rose, brushing tears off her cheeks. A few other people stood still with bowed heads, but most had wandered off to continue the evening's activities.

Soonie looked for Molly, but instead her eyes fell on Lone Warrior, sitting under the same tree where Brother Jenkins had been that first Sunday. The firelight gleamed on his twin buffalo horns. He raised an eyebrow when their eyes met.

Has he been watching me? Not that she felt embarrassed, she never cared about what other people thought of her worship practices.

Removing a few twigs from her skirt, she picked up a bowl of soup and went over to him, all the time wondering what drew her there. *Why would I offer myself up for more ridicule?* But she couldn't stop her mouth from opening. "I thought you might be hungry." The cup of soup was suddenly burning her fingers as she held it out to him.

"Thank you." He took it, but did not eat, just stared at the food as though he didn't know what it was.

"I enjoyed watching the dance. I've never seen anything like it before. So beautiful," she said.

"I'm surprised you would think so." His mouth was set in its normal hard line.

"Lone Warrior, I want to be here. I love to learn about both the Comanche and Kiowa cultures. This has been a most wonderful time in my life. Sometimes I believe . . . I may never return to Bastrop."

What force compels me to hold out my heart, when it could be so easily destroyed?

The Kiowa man raised a filled spoon a few inches, but let the liquid dribble back into the bowl. A silence fell between them, the weight of things left unsaid heavy and dark.

Finally, he dropped the spoon back into the broth. "You say you wish to be like us. Look at you! Led by what you believe to be proper." His hand holding the bowl shook. "Could you ever understand our ways? The Comanche part of you is like poison to the whites. The white side of you will never find trust in this place."

"I thought things had changed with us. You saved my life." The lumps in her throat were turning to words and she wanted to reach out and snatch them back as they tumbled out.

For an instant, a wistful light crept into his eyes. Then once more, his features hardened, like clay in an oven. He rose to his feet, and stared down at her. "I've seen you talk to the preacher. He thinks we are animals. You will join him, I think. I thought you were a spy, but now I understand what you really want. You came to make us like them."

He poured the soup out on the ground and stalked away.

Soonie had never seen anyone in the camp waste food. The puddle of liquid shimmered on the dirt, and then soaked in, leaving only a damp spot with a few potatoes and chunks of meat creating their own tiny islands.

Her feet dug into the sand, and then found the solid rock as she stumbled away from the settlement and out towards the corral.

Most of the horses were gathered in the corner, huddled together for warmth in the brisk evening air.

Stone Brother broke away from the herd and trotted toward her. He whinnied loudly and nodded his head. His tongue inched out to taste the salty tears pouring down her cheeks.

She turned her face away. "Oh Stone Brother, what will I do? Perhaps I don't belong here. But I can't go home. The children are learning so much. They need me. I can't leave, but how can I stay?" She dropped her voice to a whisper. "He's here. And he hates me so much!"

Stone Brother snorted and rolled his eyes.

"I know, I shouldn't even be thinking about him. He cares so little for his own life and safety. He risks his mind to take the Peyote. If only he could move past these things . . . he could be a great man."

Then a thought blindsided her with such force she almost sank to her knees. *Lone Warrior is right. I AM trying to change him.*

"Soonie, do you trust me?" A voice came, clear and bright in her mind, and she knew God was speaking to her. "Give the matter over to me. You know I am the only one who can save Lone Warrior. I created him, and I love him."

"Oh God, you love him even more than I do." Her breath caught in her throat. *I love him.* Tears fell faster now, sliding down to pool into her shawl until the fabric was drenched.

The huge tongue flicked close to her face, and she pushed away the golden muzzle. "Stop trying to lick me, you silly horse." She straightened up and laughed shakily. *All right, I've had my cry. I will trust God to take care of this. There's nothing else to do.*

Peace flooded through her heart, and she felt lighter, the way she always did when she finally gave things over to her Father.

A lantern bobbed towards her. "Soonie, what on earth are you doing out here, with only the moonlight?" Molly blinked when she saw her tears. "Oh, you must miss your home and family. Two months is a long time to be away."

Soonie didn't bother to try to correct her. *Father, please help me get through this. All I'm doing is hurting myself.* She shook her head at her own absurdity as they walked back towards home.

14
Journey to Town

Red dust puffed around Stone Brother's hooves and settled on his sides to mix with sweat, turning his white splotches a dull, rust color. For the first time in her life, Soonie wished for a proper carriage. *Closed in, with curtains over the windows. I'm going to be filthy by the time we reach the town to meet Doctor Early, with nothing to change into and nowhere to wash.*

Leaves scampered across the path, and Soonie shivered. The air had grown colder during the morning. Fall had finally settled in.

Molly began a trail song, probably written by some lonely cowboy on a starry night.

Roll on, roll on;
Roll on, little dogies, roll on, roll on,

Soonie and Uncle Isak joined in.

Roll on, roll on;
Roll on, little dogies, roll on, roll on

They sang until Brother Jenkins pulled up his horse and turned around in the saddle. "It's not proper to sing songs unless they are directed to the Almighty."

The impromptu choir fell silent. Molly leaned toward Soonie. "Where in the Bible did he read that?" she murmured.

Soonie shrugged.

Molly and Soonie both wore calico dresses and straw bonnets. Uncle Isak had also donned a homespun jacket and trousers, and his long braids were hidden under his hat, like on their first trip.

They had traveled since the sun rose, and it followed them across the plains. The road led them through bluffs and hills, and then would flatten out for miles, the horizon only interrupted by clumps of brush and mesquite.

When Captain Wilkerson had been told of Brother Jenkins's plans, he'd granted them permission to go, but also gave a warning. "Try not to draw attention to yourselves. If people know you're with Brother Jenkins, they'll probably think he brought you along to help with mission work and not give you a second glance. But better to be safe than to end up back at Fort Sill, or in prison."

Brother Jenkins slowed his horse until Stone Brother caught up with him.

Soonie reluctantly matched her pace to his. *I'd better try to be nice. After all, the man did change his schedule to accompany us to this meeting.* "Thank you for agreeing to help Molly. She's been so excited to meet with Doctor Early."

Brother Jenkins shrugged. "I've never stopped at this town. Even the tiny border villages need the Lord, and I might as well preach a sermon or two where I'm able. I have to say, Molly is a bright little thing. She could pick up some skills for the settlement folks. It sounds like she's already been a great help to the sick and injured."

Maybe he really does care about improving the people's situation. "Molly does have a gift for healing," Soonie said. "My foot wouldn't have mended nearly as well if it weren't for her care."

At last, buildings appeared on the road's sides. First one or two, and then several clustered together. Some sagged with age, while a few glowed with new coats of whitewash.

Brother Jenkins turned to Molly, Soonie and Uncle Isak. "Like Captain Williams said, folks probably won't pay you any mind as long as you're with me." He puffed out his chest a little. "This white collar's almost as good as a sheriff's badge."

"We certainly won't be running off on our own." With her half-Swedish heritage and her dress and bonnet, Soonie knew she probably wouldn't have any trouble.

Molly's hands trembled slightly, and she stared down at the reins.

Soonie patted her shoulder. "Don't worry. We walk with God. He will protect us."

"I know." Molly looked up quickly. "I'll try not to be afraid. I'm so excited to meet Dr. Early, I can barely stay in my saddle."

The street grew wider, and the buildings more orderly. They passed a butcher's shop. Offerings in the window looked less than fresh and buzzed with flies. Several old men sitting on wooden boxes and barrels outside the general store nodded to them as they rode past.

"This is the only town in the area with a shop like that, besides the one where your slates are coming from," said Uncle Isak. "And I've heard it's the only town for fifty miles with a saloon."

He gestured to a false-fronted building painted in garish colors. Two women stood outside.

Molly's mouth fell open. "They're only wearing underclothes!" she gasped.

Soonie's cheeks warmed. Though Bastrop had a saloon, 'loose women' were not allowed to stand around where they could be seen.

She nudged Molly. "Come on, we don't want to be left out in the street alone." But she couldn't help glancing back at the women. One smiled brazenly, but her eyes were red and black shadows lay beneath them.

"May God have mercy on their sinful souls," Brother Jenkins murmured.

He pointed to a square, gray building across the street. It bore a sign with the words 'Town Hall' scrawled across it in shaky letters. "Doctor Early told me she'd be running her clinic there. She'll be ready to meet with you ladies around noon." He pulled his pocket watch from his vest. "That'll be about an hour from now."

The group followed the pastor to a hitching post, where they dismounted and tied up their horses. The beasts lowered tired heads into the public troughs, guzzling the water greedily.

Soonie stamped her feet to get the pins and needles out. She peered down into the water, trying to pat her hair back into order beneath her straw bonnet.

"Don't be silly. The doctor knows we've just finished half a day's ride." Molly chided her.

"Still . . . oh, what's the use." Soonie turned away from the trough and followed the rest of the group.

Brother Jenkins led them to the building, where several patients lined the wall. An elderly man leaned on a cane. A Mexican woman carrying a baby had two little girls clutching her skirts, and two other women who were obviously 'in a family way' as Grandma would say, stood at the end of the porch.

The little girls, both with tangled hair and stained, torn dresses, stared out at Soonie from their fabric refuge.

"I trust you ladies will be all right here for a while?" Brother Jenkins said. "Isak and I are going to find the place where we're supposed to stay the night. The school master here is a benefactor for my fellowship and he's allowing us to sleep in the schoolhouse."

"I'm sure we'll be fine," Soonie replied.

Molly found a wooden crate and settled down, arranging her voluminous skirts around her. "I've never worn a dress with this much fabric before. What a waste! I could make a whole other gown with this."

Wonder how she would feel about the green velvet dress I wore to the holiday dance last year. Pretty as that outfit had been, Soonie hated how constricted and bundled it made her feel. Even the simple gown she wore today felt tight and strange compared to the light, loose-fitting Comanche-style clothes she had become accustomed to.

The baby was asleep now. The two little girls sat on the faded porch steps, playing a game with sticks.

The door opened and a man stepped out, broad-brimmed hat in hand. "Thank you kindly, Doctor Early."

A short woman in a crisp white apron came behind him. Her cheeks were red and round with smiles, and her sharp, intelligent eyes softened when she spoke. "Don't you be chasing those cows any more, Mr. Hollister. You let those strapping sons of yours do the heavy work, you hear?"

Mr. Hollister grinned and gestured with a bandaged hand. "A farmer's work ain't over till he's dead." His boots clattered on the wooden floor as he left.

The elderly man rose to his feet and shuffled over to the door. Doctor Early peered down the line and caught Soonie's eye. "You must be the girls who came to speak with me today. I hoped you could make the trip. I'll be finished with these folks in about thirty minutes if you don't mind waiting."

"Not at all," Soonie replied.

Doctor Early gestured to the woman with the baby, who called to the little girls. They all disappeared inside the building.

Molly gripped the sides of her box. "I can't believe we're here!" she whispered to Soonie. "She looks so ... so capable. Doesn't she look capable, Soonie?"

"Yes, she does." Soonie couldn't help but share Molly's excitement. But how could Doctor Early possibly help a Comanche girl realize her dream?

"I could help our people so much more if I could only receive the proper training," Molly twisted a bonnet string around her finger.

Soonie glanced at the closed door. Perhaps, miraculously, Doctor Early would have an answer.

The noon sun blazed over the small town before the last patient came out of the battered white door.

"Indian summer," Grandpa always called late warm spells, though he'd never explained where the term had come from.

Grandpa. Soonie's thoughts drifted to home and she pulled out a letter from she'd received earlier in the week. It had come in a packet Uncle Isak had picked up at the fort, only the second time Soonie had heard from home in almost three months. The letter was already creased and smudged from many readings.

Dear Soonie,

Remember the old rope swing hanging over the gully in the woods? Even as proper young ladies we would climb on it and swing out over the open space. I suppose those days are behind me now, as I grow ever rounder. The other day, while I was making corn bread, I burst into tears. Wylder came over to ask me what was wrong, and I couldn't give him a reason. I feel like everything is changing so quickly. And sometimes I'm afraid. What if something goes wrong, like what happened to Mama?

Grandma Louise told me later that women in my condition often became sad for no reason at all. Isn't that strange, Soonie? I don't remember my mother acting sad when she was expecting Orrie. But Wylder was so loving about it. He's so happy, Soonie. Even happier than he was on our wedding day.

Soonie folded the letter and placed it back in her handbag. Wylder and Zillia were the happiest young couple she had ever known. She smiled. *I had a feeling they'd be perfect for each other. Took them long enough to figure it out.*

Lone Warrior and his friends had left last week to hunt in the deserted hills, despite Brave Storm's fear that the trappers could still return with reinforcements. She hadn't seen Lone Warrior since the night of the fire dance.

She thought of that look on his face, the one where the corners of his mouth turned up ever so slightly. At first she thought it was a self-satisfied smirk, but now she knew better. She'd seen him give the same smile to Timothy when he was especially proud of something the boy had done, and to Brave Storm, during rare moments when they were at peace. He'd given her this expression of fondness twice now. When she'd helped him during the race, and again that night on the ridge when she'd touched his hand.

Must I think about this again? He's convinced I care for Brother Jenkins, and nothing could be further from the truth. She covered her face with her fingers. *How can I show him? How can I make him see?*

The door creaked open, interrupting her thoughts. Once more, Doctor Early emerged from the building, wiping her hands with a cloth. "Well, girls, shall we find a shady place? The town provides my lunch, and there's plenty to share." She reached behind the door and picked up a basket, which she held out invitingly.

"Sounds wonderful." Soonie's stomach grumbled in response to the tantalizing smell of fresh bread and baked ham coming from the basket. After the settlement's meager rations, they would have a feast.

The two girls followed the older woman to a patch of grass beneath a tree.

Doctor Early spread out a blanket and began to arrange food on the cloth. "I always eat outside when I come here. The clinic room gets so hot by this time and the saloon is the only place to purchase a meal. Not a proper establishment for ladies at all, even us wild ones." She winked at Soonie and Molly.

"Now, girls," she lowered her voice. "Brother Jenkins has not given me details about where you come from, but I figure you have journeyed a long, dangerous path to meet me. I'm interested to hear what you have to say."

Molly finally spoke. "Could you first please tell us a little bit about yourself? I've never heard of a woman becoming a doctor, and I wonder why you chose to come to Fort Sill."

"It would be my pleasure." Doctor Early settled on the corner of the blanket. "This weather is pretty warm for October, isn't it?" She fanned herself with her apron. "Of course, I was born and raised in Connecticut, and we might have had snow by now."

"How long have you been in Oklahoma?" Molly asked.

"Let's see." The doctor pursed her lips. "I received a doctor's certificate in the year of 1882. Then I worked in the slums of New York among the poorest of the poor for a long time." The doctor chuckled. "I once had a gentleman pay me a single postage stamp for delivering his wife's child."

Molly clasped her hands together. "You must have seen so much."

Doctor Early pulled at a loose thread on her otherwise immaculate apron. "Yes, I certainly did. And I found the most poverty-stricken people were sometimes the most beautiful."

Soonie thought of the women in the settlement who sewed bits of painted bone to tattered buckskin. She nodded.

"About a year ago," the doctor continued, "a man came by the building in Harlem where our group of women operated. He brought news of the Fort Sill reservation and showed us photographs of the people. I looked into the sad, haunted eyes staring from the pictures and knew I belonged with them. So I saved my pennies, found a few religious sponsors, and took a train.

"When I reached the reservation, the children poured out to meet me. I fell in love with them, right there on the spot."

Soonie smiled. *Exactly like me.*

"So I stayed. I've had to fight my way through traditions and mistrust, but most of the people hold at least a grudging respect for me, since I have saved many of their lives."

"How are the conditions?" Soonie asked.

Doctor Early lowered her eyes. "It's not a happy place. The government is supposed to provide money for food, clothing and supplies, but the people still don't have enough. Chief Quanah works hard for their rights and has devised ways to earn money from cattlemen driving herds through the reservation, but the need is still great. I've spent much of the meager funds given for my own provisions to buy food for the children. When I come to small towns like these, they take up a collection for me. Every penny helps."

While they ate the delicious lunch, Doctor Early shared stories about broken bones, babies born, and illnesses fought.

Soonie found herself wishing they could stay all day.

Doctor Early paused her story-telling to pat her mouth with a cloth napkin from the basket.

Molly said, "Doctor Early, do you think there's a chance . . . a chance I could become a doctor?"

The doctor's merry eyes darkened, and she rubbed her chin. "I'm not sure. Since you wrote to me, I've given the matter some thought. For a woman of any background a doctor's certificate is very difficult to obtain. I received mine at an all-women's college, where ladies had to fight long and hard to have the right to study the same subjects as men. Have either of you ever heard of a woman named Doctor La Fresche?"

The girls shook their heads.

"She's from the Omaha people, born on a reservation. She graduated from the Woman's College in Pennsylvania in 1886, just a few years ago. Now she serves as the doctor for the Omaha reservation." She brightened. "So I would say the answer is yes, Molly. It is possible."

From a pocket in her apron, she pulled out a paper and pencil. "I would like to find out more about you, so I can send a proper letter to an instructor from my old school. He might have a notion of how we could proceed."

"Of course," said Molly. "What would you like to know?"

15
Darla

While Doctor Early questioned Molly about her training and the grades she had received while at the reservation's school, Soonie's mind wandered. Blinking, she sat up straight in attempt to keep from dozing off, but the rich food and warm afternoon were taking their effect. She stood and stretched.

The side wall of the saloon shone between the trunks of the thin stand of trees shading their picnic spot. She was surprised the town would allow such a place to flourish.

While she mulled this over, the scandalous woman who had smiled at her earlier appeared around the corner. The lady put one slender hand on her hip and with the other, wiped a brow beaded with sweat.

Soonie remembered the passage of scripture where Jesus said, "I was thirsty, and you gave me something to drink." She snatched a cup of water from the lunch blanket, picked her way through the bushes, and walked over to the lady.

Up close, the woman looked younger than Soonie had first supposed; only twenty-one or so. She wore a skimpy red chemise.

"Would you like some water?" Soonie held out the drink.

The woman's darkened eyebrows shot up to her fiercely curled bangs, and her red, painted lips puckered into an 'O.' "What do you think you're doing over here, Miss? Most women wouldn't be caught within fifty feet of this place. And they'd rather die than speak to a saloon girl." She fluttered a fan made of feathers in front of her face. "But I'd bet your husband might come by."

Soonie frowned. "I don't have a husband. You looked tired, and I thought you might like something to drink."

"Oh. Well then." The girl took the glass, tried a sip of water and wrinkled her nose. "Don't drink much plain water any more. Kind of refreshing, ain't it?" She held out her other hand. "My name's Darla, by the way."

"Susannah . . . Soonie Eckhart." Soonie shook her hand. The absurdity of the conversation hit her and she bit back a giggle.

Darla didn't seem to notice. "Say, you aren't looking for a job, are you? Pretty girl like you wouldn't have a problem. The boss man ain't here right now, but he'll be back soon." She bent a little closer and Soonie caught a whiff of overly-sweet perfume. "If you ask me though, you'd be better slogging in the field or cookin' in a hot kitchen than working for Mr. Gandro."

"No, I'm not looking for a job." Soonie hoped her face didn't betray her shock at the implication. She didn't want to hurt this lady's feelings. The girl probably already dealt with her share of rude people.

"Umm Hmm." Darla stared at the road over Soonie's shoulder.

"Well, have a nice day." Soonie turned to leave, but a familiar voice from around the front of the saloon made her heart skip a beat.

"Boys, y'all get those horses put up. I'm gonna whet my whistle."

Darla's eyes widened. "I know that voice. That man is pure evil."

"I recognize it too," Soonie whispered back. "And yes, he is." She scrunched up against the wall and peeked around the corner.

It was Hal all right; there was no mistaking that evil grin and shock of white hair. He'd paused to read a sign by the saloon door. "No spurs or spittin', huh? We'll see about that, right boys?" He threw back his head and guffawed as he walked into the saloon.

I can't believe he's here. Soonie's heart thudded against her chest while she inched back around the wall.

Molly sat with Doctor Early less than fifty feet away, in plain view. The hitching post Hal's men were gathered around had nothing in front of it. If one of them turned and looked . . . if they saw Molly . . .

I can't run over and warn her, they'd be sure to notice. Oh God, what should I do? Maybe they won't recognize us in these clothes. Should I risk it?

The saloon girl had made her way almost to the end of the building, and was beckoning to her. "Come over here," she hissed. "There's a shed out back where some of us girls hide when Mr. Gandro gets too drunk."

Soonie shuddered. The perils of a saloon girl's life had never been something she'd thought about. She gestured towards Molly. "I can't leave my friend. Those men have reason to do us great harm if they find out we are here."

The eyebrows shot up again. Darla shrugged. "Your business, dear. I don't need to know any more about it. Here." She unwound a black mantilla draped around her waist, revealing a pair of scandalous lace pantaloons. "Put this shawl over your hat. Lots of the ladies in town wear dark veils to prevent freckling."

"Oh, thank you so much!" Soonie took the veil and covered her straw bonnet and face. Perhaps she looked ridiculous, but it was the best plan they had. "What about you? You can't walk around like that!"

Darla put her hands on her hips. "Silly girl. I think you know what I am. Now go over and warn your friend. Be safe." She darted off towards the back of the saloon in a flurry of red crepe and lace, bright yellow ringlets bobbing around her shoulders.

Pulling the mantilla closer, Soonie forced herself to walk back through the trees at a normal pace and tried not to glance toward the hitching post or the saloon. The streets were full of people, and she couldn't distinguish one voice from another. The world looked strange through the filtered lace of her mantilla. Though shrouded, she felt more exposed than Darla.

After an agonizing walk back through the trees, she slid next to Molly on the blanket. "Molly, turn around and duck your head," she said in a low voice.

Molly jumped, and her eyes widened. "Soonie, I didn't recognize . . . you startled me! Why are you wearing that?"

"Don't look behind you, Molly," Soonie whispered. "Hal and his men are here. We must leave at once."

Molly's hand crept up to her mouth. "Oh no." Her voice lowered to a whisper. "What can we do?"

Concern filled Doctor Early's eyes. "What seems to be the trouble, girls?"

Soonie rose from the blanket. "We don't have time to tell the story. We have to find my uncle and get out of town."

Doctor Early stood as well. "Surely you can stay until supper. And don't you have lodging for the night? The ride here was so long."

Soonie darted a look at the front of the saloon. No sign of Hal's men for the moment, but they could come out of the building at any time. "Brother Jenkins arranged for us to stay with the school master, but we really mustn't. I can't explain right now."

Molly's shoulders stiffened, and Soonie could tell she was fighting the urge not to turn around and check the street for herself.

Doctor Early held out her hand. "Well girls, come on then. You can stay in the town hall until your uncle gets back. I'll come out and clean up lunch in a moment."

"But if they find us in there, we'll be trapped," Molly protested.

The older woman placed her hand over Molly's trembling fingers. "Don't worry. I have more powerful tools in my bag than a stethoscope."

Feeling safer in her mantilla, Soonie couldn't resist one backward glance at the saloon as she followed Doctor Early into the building. Was that Darla's face peering through the bushes? She blinked and the face disappeared.

Doctor Early led them into the main room which was empty and hot. Rows of crude wooden benches led up to a podium at the front. Small squares of light settled on the floor, let in by windows close to the ceiling. A spider scurried over the rough wooden slats on some tiny mission.

The doctor closed the door. "Ladies, I will have to leave you here while I fetch your uncle. Now, these men you are afraid of don't know you are in town. Is that correct?"

Soonie shook her head. "I don't know how they could. I think it's just a terrible coincidence. Our encounter with them happened at least a day's ride from this place. But if they see Uncle Isak, they might recognize him as a Comanche and get suspicious."

"We'll figure out a way to get him here so no one sees him. Will you be all right while I'm gone?"

Soonie pulled out her dagger from the hidden sheath in her skirts, just enough for Doctor Early to see the hilt. "We have this."

"Good. I'll return as fast as I'm able."

The door clicked behind her.

Soonie stood on her tiptoes to look out the window. The trees in front of the building were too thick here; she couldn't see past them to the street. *I'm silly to panic. They can't possibly realize we are here. Doctor Early will warn Uncle Isak. We'll leave town and no one will know.*

The young man's face, cold and dead with wide, staring eyes, flashed into her mind. A thought which had been working its way into the murky memories of that day pushed through, like a splinter shoved into skin. He had called Hal . . . "Pa," she murmured.

"What?" Molly's head snapped up.

"Nothing. I hope we get away soon."

"Me too. Oh Soonie, I never thought we'd see those men again. I wish we hadn't come! I've put you and Isak in terrible danger." Molly's lip trembled.

Placing a hand on the girl's shoulder, Soonie said, "You're worth it, Molly. You have greatness inside of you, and the ability to do so much for your people. God will keep us safe."

She stood to look out the window once more.

Scarlet and yellow flashed through the trees. *Darla?* Soonie strained to see better. The girl moved up the porch.

Soonie went to the door.

Molly drew back. "What are you doing?"

"It's all right. She's my friend." Soonie pulled open the latch.

Darla squeezed inside, and then slammed the door. A fresh red mark bloomed on her pale cheek, and tears brightened the corners of her eyes.

"My boss made me go in and serve those oafs." She wiped her cheeks. "I've met lots of idiot men in my time, but those fellas . . ." she placed a fluttering hand over her heart. "Well, I'm sure you nice ladies don't want to hear about that."

"We've encountered them as well," said Molly. "We won't have a fit of vapors if you tell us."

Darla's eyes widened. "They drank down some whiskey mighty quick, then that Hal got to talking. Said some injuns killed his son." She peered at Soonie. "Are you injun?"

"Part," Soonie tapped her fingers against her chin. "So what happened?"

"He said he'd been up by Fort Sill on a hunting trip. He went by the reservation to see if he recognized anyone, but the soldiers ran him and his men off. Then he'd been asking around, and he caught word of an injun settlement a ways from here . . . a secret one. He's tryin' to recruit enough men to flush 'em out. Says he'll pay cold, hard cash to anyone who helps find the folks who killed his son."

Drops of sweat poured down Soonie's forehead and stung her eyes. "Molly, we have to tell the sheriff. Maybe he would believe our side of the story and help us."

"Oh, my stars and heavens!" Darla clutched her hands together. "Sheriff Winters is kin to Hal! He'll lock you up, sure as sure. Rumor is that Hal's been bribing the sheriff to let him do as he wishes. Hal's pretty rich, he trades with a fur dealer who comes in from the east."

Rocks crunched outside the building and Soonie peered out the window.

A wagon clattered into the yard with Doctor Early driving. A canvas covered the back. The doctor jumped down, tied the horse to the porch rail, and peered around the yard before lifting the covering.

Uncle Isak crept out, and he and the doctor hurried towards the building.

Soonie turned to the saloon girl. "Darla, it looks like they're here. Thank you so much for warning us. And here's your shawl."

"You're welcome." Darla dabbed her face with the cloth. "Oooh, the saloon boss'll kill me dead for leaving those men all lonesome."

Soonie touched her shoulder. "Come with us, then."

Darla's lips formed a smile, but her eyes grew weary, and looked as old as Grandmother Eagle's. "No, I'd better stay here, where I belong." Her blue eyes searched Soonie's face, then Molly's. "I don't care what anyone says about savage Comanches. You girls are true ladies."

"And so are you," Soonie replied.

Darla stepped through the door and was gone.

16
Escape

Evening had coaxed the moon over the silent town before Uncle Isak was convinced it would be safe to leave the small white building.

"Hal doesn't have an army organized yet," he told the frightened girls. "For all we know, it might just be a drunk man talking big."

Molly picked up a piece of bread from the supper Doctor Early had brought them, stared at the crumbling crust for a moment, then put it back down. She looked up. "If the sheriff is really on Hal's side, he could convince the townspeople to join the search party,"

Uncle Isak bowed his head. "True."

The dark patch of sky in the windows brightened as the moon rose. Uncle Isak got up from his chair. "Let's go. If we are travelling by night, then we need to be able to see the road."

Brother Jenkins and Doctor Early had already said their goodbyes. They needed to rest before their journey to Fort Sill on the morrow, and Uncle Isak didn't want anyone to know they were associated with them in case trouble did arise.

The group of three slipped out of the building and into the darkened street. The thick scent of manure and stagnant water rose to meet them.

Lively fiddle music and laughter came from the direction of the saloon. A few dogs raised shaggy heads to watch as they passed by homes and storefronts. Otherwise the town was quiet.

Uncle Isak led the way to an alley behind the building. "Brother Jenkins said he'd move the horses to the stable by the schoolhouse. That way no one would wonder who they belonged to."

"Or steal them," Molly muttered.

Rocks crunching beneath Soonie's feet sounded like a mule eating oats. *If only I had my moccasins. Why do women even wear these ridiculous shoes?* She picked at her corset, which had been digging into her ribs all day. *No, I haven't missed wearing town clothes one bit.*

Finally, they reached the stable. Uncle Isak glided through the doors and brought out their horses, one by one.

Soonie patted Stone Brother's nose. "Let's get home, boy."

His ear bent back to catch her whisper, and he whinnied softly.

The moon was full and shining, like a new dollar coin from the bank.

The horses' hooves sent up clouds of dust in the moonlight.

Soonie didn't see the crumpled form by the side of the road, but Stone Brother did. He snorted and reared his head back.

"Uncle Isak," she cried. She slid off her horse and ran to the girl's side. "It's Darla!"

Darla peered up through her mantilla. "Soonie? I figured you'd be by. Can I ride with you, just until we reach a town where I can stay? I can't work for that man anymore." She pushed the cloth back, and Soonie saw a thin stream of blood trickling from a cut on her forehead. "Work's not worth dying for. I'll figure out some other way to fill my belly."

Uncle Isak dismounted and joined Soonie. "You'll have to both ride Stone Brother," he said. "If you're the girl who helped Soonie and Molly earlier, you know the danger we're in."

"I don't care." Darla stuck out her chin and rose to shaky feet. "And I have my own horse." She disappeared behind a clump of trees and came back, leading a skinny, but capable-looking beast. "I didn't steal him," she answered their questioning looks. "Won him in a poker game awhile back."

"I should look at that cut," Molly reached out to touch it.

Darla turned her head away. "It's fine, I've had worse." She climbed on her horse and clucked to him. "Come on, Jimmy."

The group set off again, making good time in the cool night.

They'd only journeyed for half an hour when they saw the glow of firelight from the side of the road.

Uncle Isak raised his hand. "I was afraid of this. With no boarding house in the town, Hal and his men would have to camp in the outskirts. I hoped they'd still be at the saloon."

"No, they left before I snuck out," said Darla. "Hal said they wanted to make an early start tomorrow."

"Maybe it's not them," said Molly. "It could be anyone, really."

"I need to be sure," said Uncle Isak. "The road here is wide and clear, we can travel through this pass just fine in the moonlight. But going around, through the woods, in the dark would be foolish. This land is full of cougars, maybe even a bear or two." He slid off his horse. "You girls stay here behind these rocks. I remember Hal and his men from that time in the canyon well enough, I'm going to find out if they're here."

"Be careful," Soonie said to his retreating form.

The moonlight spilled out over the wide, open road. "If we crossed here, we could be seen for quite a ways," Molly whispered.

Darla shrugged and patted her horse's scraggly mane. "Bet Jimmy could outrun any of those fellows."

Uncle Isak returned swiftly, his eyes dark with worry. "It's Hal all right, and he's gathered some friends. Eight men, two keeping watch. We'll have to take another path."

"Or we could create a diversion." Molly's voice was cold.

"I thought of that, but . . . " Uncle Isak's eyes shifted to Soonie and Darla.

Most of her life, Soonie had been seen as the strong one, the most practical, the bravest. In school, the teachers had always asked her to remove bugs and critters that wandered into the room. Friends came to her for advice and help. *I feel like a five-year-old child.* She held out her hands. "What can I do?"

"You and Darla hold the horses." Isak scanned the road. "Molly and I will return as quickly as possible."

"Give me a moment." Molly went behind a rock. Skirts rustled. In a moment, she stepped out in her petticoats, barefooted. Her borrowed dress was bunched in her hands. "I can't run in those clothes."

"Are you sure you should do this?" Soonie asked Uncle Isak. "Is it worth the risk?"

"I know Hal pretty well," Darla broke in. "The man is a brute and if he already has a bone to pick with you, he won't need another reason to cause you some hurt. And a man died in these woods last week. They found him black and swollen from a rattlesnake bite."

Molly squeezed Soonie's hand. "Pray for us." She and Uncle Isak slipped off into the night.

Soonie looked over at Darla. The girl still hadn't cleaned the dried blood from her nose, and the red mark was turning purple. She was biting her lip, and her eyes were wide.

"Don't worry." Soonie tried to sound brave. "Isak and Molly will come up with a way to get us through this. And I know you'll be welcome at the settlement for as long as you need to stay. We don't have much, but there's food and shelter, at least."

Her own heart pounded in her chest, despite her words. She stared out through a crack in the rocks, towards the fires. Her fingers found her knife's hilt and she gripped it until the tips were sore.

Seek me, came the voice in her heart. *Seek me first.*

Of course. Soonie sagged against the rock and clasped her hands together. "God, please, please direct Uncle Isak and Molly's path. They don't want to harm anyone. We just need to get home safely. Please."

Darla's eyes were closed and her head was bowed as well.

Soonie remembered the young man. She shook her head. "Please don't let anyone get hurt, including the horses."

Rising to her feet, Soonie strained to hear any noise, any clue of what was going on. From this distance, she would only be able to hear the loudest shouts.

She pictured the two dark shapes, creeping across the rocks silent as death.

The two guards wouldn't be expecting a disturbance. They'd most likely be drinking or blinding themselves by staring into the fire.

Molly might be hiding in the bushes to keep watch, while Uncle Isak would probably slip down the line of trees to slice the horses' tethers . . .

A thunder of hooves split the night wide open. Shouts and curses joined the sounds, moving in the opposite direction of the road.

Darla stood, frozen with one hand over her mouth. Soonie pushed her towards her horse.

"I can't, I can't ride out there in the open, I'll be shot!" Darla wailed.

Soonie all but picked the girl up and threw her on the beast. She yanked the other horses' reins from the tree trunk where they had been tied. "Here." She shoved them at Darla. Then she climbed on Stone Brother and took the reins back from the frightened girl. This whole operation took less than a minute, but she felt as though she were wading through molasses.

As Soonie led the horses forward, two gliding forms appeared on the road. She dug her heels into Stone Brother's side and he sped up.

When she passed Molly and Isak, she slowed so they could grab the reins from her hand. In an instant, all four horses were galloping down the road.

A loud crack came from behind them, and something whistled past Soonie's head. Darla screamed.

Someone is shooting. They are shooting at us. We could die tonight.

"Run, run," she hissed, laying low against Stone Brother's neck. She pressed her knees tighter and he responded with a burst of speed. After that, the world became a swirl of darkness and moon spots and unending jolts from the rise and fall of hooves beneath her. Her own breath burned the air around her, singeing her skin.

At long last, the horses slowed. Uncle Isak turned back to them and let out a whoop.

The hairs on Soonie's neck stood on end. *He really is as wild as Lone Warrior.*

Uncle Isak grinned widely. "It's good to feel dangerous again. Just for once."

An answering whoop came from the trees, and the girls looked around.

Darla's hair had tumbled around her shoulders, and she clutched the reins like the horse was the only thing keeping her from certain death. "That was as scary as a graveyard on All Hallows Eve," she breathed.

Molly nodded.

Cactus Pear stepped from beneath the trees, with Lone Warrior on her back. The horses whinnied greetings to each other.

"Hello," said Lone Warrior.

Soonie placed a hand over her heart, then glared at the betraying fingers and pretended like she was dusting off her blouse.

Lone Warrior studied Soonie. "You aren't injured? Molly? Who is this other white girl?"

"I'm fine," said Molly. "But someone shot at us."

"Name's Darla, sugar plum." Darla held out a lace-gloved hand, but Lone Warrior ignored it and turned towards Uncle Isak.

"I thought something must be wrong since you were riding so fast. You weren't pursued?"

Uncle Isak shrugged. "They had no horses."

Lone Warrior stared down the path behind them. "Storm's coming to wipe out tracks, and I doubt they'll find their beasts if it thunders much."

As if to confirm his statement, clouds began to creep over the moon. The breeze that had been gentle grew stronger.

A warm glow spread through Soonie during this conversation, and her thoughts scrambled over one another in such confusion she couldn't even think of what to say. They were safe, and she hadn't realized how badly she missed Lone Warrior until now, when she saw him and her heart threatened to jump right out and run up to his horse on its own.

Lone Warrior turned to her again. "Are you sure you're all right?"

"I'm in one piece. See?" she held out her arms.

His fingers twitched, and she thought he might reach out to touch her, but he didn't.

"Why are you here, Lone Warrior?" asked Uncle Isak. "Why are you not in disguise?"

"I had no time. Timothy . . ." Lone Warrior swallowed, and his eyes hardened in the moonlight. "Timothy has been hurt."

17

Timothy

"We want to hear what happened," said Uncle Isak. "But let's continue to move. We need to get back before the storm hits." His horse stepped back out on the road, and the girls and Lone Warrior urged their mounts to follow.

"Thomas, Gray Fox and I were at the Peyote lodge to rest after a long day of hunting." Lone Warrior's shoulders slumped. "The cactus buttons help to strengthen our sleep.

"Timothy and his friends went into the lodge and ate some of the Peyote. The tipi caught on fire." Lone Warrior stared down at the reins. "The other two boys escaped. Timothy was the closest to the flames. Ah!" He brought a hand to his eyes. "The burns are so bad."

He turned in the saddle towards Soonie. "You were right. Peyote is not a gift from the Creator." His voice broke and he looked away.

Soonie longed to reach out and touch his shoulder, to comfort him in some way. But she held back. "Will Timothy be all right?"

"Grandmother Eagle has done everything in her power, but my brother is in great pain," Lone Warrior answered. "Molly, I came to find you and see if I could catch the doctor woman before she went back to Fort Sill. But I see you had to leave sooner than planned."

"Yes, Hal ended up in the same town and we had to get away," said Molly. "Doctor Early is already heading back to the reservation."

"And you can't go back through that town. Hal will recognize you for sure," said Uncle Isak.

"Ah." Lone Warrior hunched over on his horse and rapped on his chest with a fist.

"Doctor Early gave me some medicines for the settlement," said Molly. "There's a salve she said would be good for burns. We can try that when we get there."

"How long 'till we get to the place?" Darla asked.

"A few more hours," said Uncle Isak. "We've ridden the horses harder than I like to, but under the circumstances we had no choice. These animals have lived on the plains all their lives. And I must say your beast is holding his own."

"Yeah, Jimmie ain't too shabby." Darla patted the scrawny neck.

"For now, we could pray," said Soonie.

Uncle Isak prayed as they rode, then Molly.

To Soonie's shock, Lone Warrior bowed his head and prayed. "Lord God of the heavens and world, please . . ." His voice broke and he swallowed. "Please heal my brother. You have created all things. Your son, Jesus, healed everyone who asked. Please heal Timothy now. And forgive me for my foolishness."

Wonder filled Soonie's heart and she could scarcely think to stammer out her own prayer.

Only Darla remained silent.

They continued to ride, while lightning painted the sky behind them in brilliant streaks. The air grew heavy with the scent of rain, but they managed to keep in front of it.

Hours later, as the moon broke through drifting clouds; the settlement's familiar hill loomed before them.

When they'd reached the corral, Uncle Isak gestured for the girls to go on to the houses. "I'll care for the horses. They've earned extra oats this night. Lone Warrior, you and Molly see about Timothy."

Brave Storm stood outside his tipi. His face was almost covered by his robe and his arms were folded tightly around him. He looked up as Soonie, Molly, Darla and Lone Warrior approached.

"He is better," he said.

The four of them, even Darla, who had never met Timothy, breathed a collective sigh of relief.

Grandmother Eagle emerged from the tipi's opening. The first smile Soonie had ever seen her give spread across the wizened face when she saw them. "Molly." She grasped her granddaughter's hands and leaned forward until their foreheads touched.

"It's good to see you, too, Grandmother." Molly squeezed the leathered hands then stepped back. "But Timothy . . ."

The old woman's smile grew brighter. "I thought he would surely pass before the first rays of dawn. That would be very bad, for no one can find the happy hunting grounds in the dark. But a short while ago his fever broke, and he fell asleep. He is still resting now."

"This is good to hear," Molly said. "I'll go check on him." She went inside the tipi. Lone Warrior and Brave Storm followed her.

Darla tapped Soonie on the shoulder. "I feel so out of place," she whispered. "I never thought I'd be in a real injun camp. But they all seem nice."

"We are nice." Soonie laughed. "We'll go up to the shanty as soon as Molly checks on Timothy. For one thing, we'll have to find you some clothes."

Darla gasped and pulled her mantilla closer. "I forgot, I'm wearing my saloon clothes. Land sakes! These people must think I'm a sight!"

Soonie glanced around at the other homes. "At least it's still dark, and many people aren't out yet," she said. "But what are you going to do? You are welcome to stay here as long as you like, I'm sure, but . . ."

"No, honey, I'd stick out here like a June bug in a church. But I don't want to work in a saloon again." Darla's forehead wrinkled. "I'd like to try to find a job as cook somewhere. I'm a pretty good in the kitchen and it would be nice to do something respectable."

"Perhaps you can travel with Brother Jenkins to Dallas next time he comes through here. I'm sure there would be plenty of places for you to work in a big city like that."

"Maybe," Darla replied.

Molly came out of the tent. "The burns aren't so terrible. I think Timothy must have been in shock from the pain. Pain is not always bad with burns; it can mean they are mostly on the surface. From what I have studied, they're not as likely to become septic. Let's go home. I have more herbs and supplies there I might be able to use."

Soonie staggered behind her up the path to the little hut. "I could sleep all day," she moaned. "I can't wait to get out of these shoes and into my real clothes."

Molly stopped short. "Oh my goodness. I completely forgot I was only wearing my petticoats." Two bright spots appeared on her dark cheeks.

"Sugar, you and I are two peas in a pod," said Darla.

"Oh well. We're safe, and that's what matters," said Soonie.

Once in the house, Soonie hurried to the washtub behind the hanging cloth. She peeled off the soiled, stained dress and scrubbed layers of dirt from her skin.

What was happening with Lone Warrior? His mumbled prayer had been sincere, and had been directed to the God of the Universe that she also prayed to, and not some mythical entity. *Is God truly working a change in his heart? Or is it just something I'm imagining because I want it to happen so badly?*

Soft chanting met Soonie's ears as she approached Brave Storm's tipi. The Kiowa man was sitting outside, with his eyes closed and hands raised toward the setting sun.

She waited a long time, until he finally stopped and opened his eyes.

"Brave Storm, may I go in?" she asked.

He grunted his permission, closed his eyes, and continued his prayer.

Soonie slipped through the flap. The usual acrid smell of the tipi had been replaced by the much more pleasing aroma of the chamomile salve Molly had used to hasten the healing process.

Lone Warrior sat cross-legged on one side of the tent, with a worn book opened in his lap.

"Is he asleep?" Soonie nodded to the bed.

"Yes, but he has been that way for a while. He will be hungry, so his belly might wake him soon."

Soonie crept to Lone Warrior's side and peeked at the book.

"Why . . . you're reading Matthew," she gasped. The browned pages bore scrawled notes and many verses were underlined.

The spectacles Lone Warrior was wearing somehow fit with the beaded vest and bone jewelry. He wasn't wearing his porcupine cap.

"Yes. It's my favorite of the gospels. It has been a few years since I've read this book." He smiled wryly. "I somehow got the idea that eating cactus would help me talk to God more effectively."

"How long have you studied the Bible?" Soonie asked.

He closed the book and rubbed his chin. "I became a believer when I was ten years old. But after a time, I moved away from the scriptures. I thought I'd found a better road. But it's like you said. 'Narrow is the way to righteousness, but wide is the path to destruction.'"

He rested his chin on his hand. "Have I told you that you're pretty? For a white girl, I mean."

"No, you haven't." Soonie played with the beads she'd woven into her hair.

"Well, you are. I've been thinking about many things, Soo-nie, ever since Timothy was hurt. Many choices I've made were based on anger and hate. I've come from a smoke-filled cave, into a new morning."

Soonie kept silent.

"I've had some talks with God. Without help from Peyote," he added. "I've asked Him to take away the darkness within me. His book," he tapped the Bible, "calls us to love one another, despite our different tribes and tongues." He covered his face with hands crisscrossed with scars. "I want Him to show me how to love people again."

"He's already begun the work, I can tell," Soonie said, lacing her fingers together to keep from reaching out to him.

"Miss Su?" Timothy's weak voice drifted from the blankets.

A pang of guilt hit Soonie. She had almost forgotten her original mission. She hurried to the young boy's side. "Hello, Timothy. I came to check on you."

The boy's smile shone through the pain written on his young face. "I'm glad. I missed you."

"I brought you something." Soonie pulled out a peppermint stick from her pocket. "It's my last secret piece. Just for you."

Timothy took it from her. "Candy." He closed his eyes. "Thank you, Miss Su. I'm glad you are here."

Soonie glanced back at Lone Warrior. He was watching them with that tiny smile of his.

She smiled back. "I'm glad to be here as well, Timothy."

18
No Choice

"All things bright and beautiful
All creatures great and small

Brother Jenkins had chosen not to travel to Fort Sill, but instead returned to the settlement to make sure the girls and Isak had made it back. Since it happened to be Sunday, he decided to go ahead and hold a service.

All things wise and wonderful,
The Lord, God, made them all."

How could such a cheerful song sound so mournful? Soonie couldn't bring herself to join in, although Darla, who stood by her side, sang with gusto.

Soonie hardly recognized the girl in the practical calico dress and collar she had lent her. But Darla's cheeks and lips were a tinge redder than a natural glow should be, and Soonie sent up a hasty prayer that Brother

Jenkins wouldn't notice. *He might pass out in front of the congregation.*

The corners of Brother Jenkin's mouth were pulled down, and his eyelids drooped.

Poor man, he's probably exhausted.

Soonie checked over the children that stood around the room. Laura and Prairie Bird were right at the front, singing in their cheerful voices. The little ones stood with their mamas. Black Turtle, Hershel and Felix sat in the corner, looking lost without their leader.

Timothy had made remarkable progress in the last two days. He stayed in bed, but the angry red skin had mostly fallen off. Molly believed that when he'd healed, only thin white scars would remain.

Uncle Isak and Brave Storm had gone out that morning to speak to Captain Wilkerson about the issue with Hal and his men, and would return to address the camp after church.

A dark foreboding filled Soonie's heart. *If Hal gathers a large group of men who are convinced we are dangerous savages, how will we protect ourselves?* Even if they did fight back, it would only bring more condemnation upon them.

The service ended after what seemed like an eternity. Soonie couldn't have repeated three words of the message to save her life, she was so distracted.

She hurried to the door, but Brother Jenkins was right there, bobbing at her elbow.

"Miss Eckhart, I'm glad to see you returned safely. I had to make sure Doctor Early made it to the next town to meet her escort, or I would have come back with you. What a dangerous journey you made." His eyes settled on her clothing. "I see you have chosen to adopt the local method of dress."

"I have always dressed like this, Brother Jenkins, except for church and school. My clothes were ruined on the trip, and therefore, unsuitable."

He blinked rapidly a few times. "I understand. Of course."

"Excuse me, please. I must find out if my uncle has returned from speaking to Captain Wilkerson."

She stepped away, but Brother Jenkins grabbed her elbow.

"Miss Eckhart . . . Susannah. I have something to discuss with you." He drew her away from the crowd.

Darla came towards them, stopped, gave a little wave, and walked off.

Soonie was tempted to pull away from his grasp. *No, I'll go along and let him have his say.*

Brother Jenkins led her around the building, and stopped beneath a tree. He tipped his hat back, and studied her with earnest eyes.

"You may think this settlement's customs are archaic, but it is far more civilized than many of the reservations I have visited. The women here are savage enough, but some of the places . . . there is little adherence to any sort of decorum. Many don't even know how to use silverware properly." His mouth pursed as though he'd tasted something sour. "They all jab with knives, even the children."

"Brother Jenkins, I really must . . ."

"No, no." He held up his hands.

"Please hear me out. I've given this matter much thought. I'm a man. These women won't listen to me, even when I've tried to explain certain changes would be for the best. But you, my dear, you could be so much more persuasive."

Soonie was too shocked to reply.

"Of course, it wouldn't do for us to travel together alone. Not with our current relationship. But if we were partners, think of the good we could do. You are strong and brave. Would you be my wife?"

Soonie slapped a hand over her mouth, afraid to let out the gasp of horror or hysterical giggle, she wasn't sure which would come. While struggling for a reply, she turned her head and saw Lone Warrior, sitting on a log a short distance from the school house. He was watching them, his face impossible to read.

A deep longing entered her heart. A sudden, striking wish that Lone Warrior would come, take her hand, and claim her for his own. She'd never met a man she trusted with her life, beyond her family.

But does he even feel the same way about me? He did say I was pretty.

"Susannah?"

She started. She had almost forgotten Brother Jenkins, who stared with the same limpid expression he almost always wore, except his eyes were just a little wider.

"Oh, Brother Jenkins, I couldn't be your wife. You can't possibly care for me. I'm—I'm just not refined enough for you. But I wish you all the best in your work and I pray that God will someday show you how to love people for who they are."

She moved away from him then, but couldn't help glancing back. He was rooted to the spot, his mouth hanging open.

Darla was waiting for her at the schoolhouse door. "What was that all about?"

"I'll tell you later," said Soonie. "Would you mind going on to lunch without me? I'll be there in a few minutes."

Darla nodded and flounced off in the direction of the fire circle.

Soonie's head warned her to follow Darla, but her heart had complete control of her legs. The betraying limbs carried her to the log where Lone Warrior sat. She sank down beside him.

"Hello." He turned and gave her a true smile.

"Hello," she answered, hardly able to look at him. *I feel like a child.* "How is Timothy?"

"Much better." Lone Warrior stood up and reached out to her. "Will you come?"

"Come? Where?"

Lone Warrior took her hand, and hot pinpricks, like sparks from a campfire, tingled through her skin. He led her back to the stream by the clay copse.

The ground was covered with fallen leaves, golden and flaming red. "I haven't been back here since, well, that day with the children," Soonie said.

"Come and sit." He brushed leaves off a rock.

"All right." She perched on the edge of the stone.

He went over to a large tree stump. Reaching inside, he pulled out a cloth bundle. He brought it over and drew back the cloth to reveal cornbread and a steaming pot of beans.

"Lunch? Did you make this?"

Lone Warrior shook his head. "Molly." He smiled. "She told me . . . you like surprises."

He asked Molly what I would like. And she helped him plan this? Soonie was touched to her very core. "I do love surprises. This is very nice. Thank you. And I will thank Molly too."

He shrugged and sat beside her. They ate in silence for a while, listening to the cardinals call through the treetops.

"The bird searches for a lover." Lone Warrior said, pointing to the flashes of red feathers.

Soonie's fingers trembled as she reached for the last square of cornbread. "Do you think he will find one?" she asked.

"I hope so." He turned back and studied her with his eyes, dark as beaver's fur.

The voices of children rang through the canyon from the schoolyard.

"Isak must be back." Lone Warrior leapt up and held out a hand to help Soonie to her feet.

She stood, and he didn't let go of her hand. He pulled her closer, and whispered.

"I was wrong to say you were pretty."

Her heart sank and she turned her head away.

"You are the most beautiful woman I have ever met."

Soonie's head swam, and a deep shuddering breath came from her very soul. She opened her mouth to say something, she wasn't sure what, but before any words could come, he dropped her hand and ran off in the direction of the school house.

"Wait for me!" Soonie called. She picked up her skirts and chased after him through the rocks and trees. They were laughing and panting when they reached the school house door.

Lone Warrior put a finger to his lips and they crept to an open place against the wall. Everyone in the settlement seemed to be there, even Grandmother Eagle, who sat like a queen despite the rough wooden chair she was perched on.

Captain Wilkerson was at the front of the room, with Uncle Isak to his right, and Brave Storm to his left. Brother Jenkins stood behind the three of them, shifting from foot to foot.

Captain Wilkerson cleared his throat. "I come before you today as a friend and ally. We have enjoyed an unlikely peace for many years. Mr. Isak has told me of your trouble with the trappers. I believe him. I would trust anything he says, for he is a man of his word." He scanned the room, his faded blue eyes moist. "I assure you, my heart is heavy with the news I must share with you today.

"The sheriff of the border town rules with a renegade hand. I've kept tabs on him for a long time, but anyone with information that could send him behind bars has been silenced with bullets or bribes. Apparently, you folks have had some bad dealings with a group of trappers near here. And one of the men is kin to the sheriff."

Soonie's heart thudded in her chest. *This is it. I've sensed a change was coming. And now it's here.*

Uncle Isak stepped forward. "We must leave. Tonight."

Murmurs filled the room. Uncle Isak's eyes flashed, and he held up his hand. Everyone quieted.

"Word has come. The trappers are on the move, with a posse of two dozen men. They convinced the town that there's a band of savages somewhere in these hills. We were hoping the rain had washed out our tracks. But Captain Wilkerson has received word they are headed in this direction. We can only guess the reason they haven't found us yet is because no one would think we'd be so close to a government fort. But they'll figure it out soon enough, and then the captain and his men will also be in trouble for aiding murderers and horse thieves."

"Both of those things were done in self-defense," Soonie whispered to Lone Warrior.

Lone Warrior nodded, and his jaw tightened. He slipped his hand over hers.

Warmth flooded through her, and her entire being filled with joy, despite the situation. She clawed her way out of the happy reverie, back to the dark mood of the schoolroom.

"We will pack what we can," Uncle Isak was saying. "Our wagons will be loaded. We'll take the long path around, back to Fort Sill. Doctor Early told me that a better school has been established there, so the children are no longer being taken away. Yes, we will give up many freedoms, but it is good to live, and not rot in prison."

Some of the women fell to their knees, moaning softly. Children stared at the adults with solemn, worried eyes and men's hands clenched into fists by their sides.

Gray Fox stepped forward. "We should fight. We have the right to be free, like all Americans."

"No, we don't," said Brave Storm. "We have already addressed this matter. If we fight, we make things worse for the reservation. And Captain Wilkerson could never allow it."

Captain Wilkerson rubbed his mustache. "I chose to help you hide away here for four years, since I owed a debt to Mr. Isak, and now, for my friendships with many of you. It is because of those friendships that I must ask you all to leave. It would pain me greatly to see one drop of blood lost from anyone here. All these young 'uns," he swept his arm out to indicate the children, "deserve to live and grow, to see what they can become."

We cannot risk this good man's reputation. Soonie squeezed Lone Warrior's hand.

Uncle Isak saw her gesture from the front of the room and his eyes widened. His mouth twitched at the corners.

Brave Storm raised his hand. "Brother Jenkins will say a prayer, and then we will go and pack."

Two wagons, three dozen horses. Twenty-eight people. How will we manage?

Brother Jenkins bowed his head. "Dear Lord, bless your children . . ." his voice wavered. Soonie peeped from between her fingers. Were those tears slipping down his cheeks?

"And may they reach their home safely. Amen."

A silence followed, broken only by sniffles and stifled sobs.

Uncle Isak began to sing in a soft tenor:

Amazing Grace
How sweet the sound . . ."

Most of the crowd joined in. The non-believers stood in respectful silence. Even Grandmother Eagle bowed her head.

The beautiful words swirled with the melody, and a peace flooded through the room. The impossible peace Soonie had come to rely on throughout her life.

Everything will work out. Somehow, we will all be safe.

19
Packing

By the time Soonie filled her small carpet bag, Molly and Grandma Eagle had packed up the rest of the house.

Darla mostly stood by with the broom and poked at anything that looked like a dust bunny. "No one's ever accused me of being a laze-around," she said. "But I truly don't know how to help. I might break something."

"I've been here for three months, and I feel just the same way," said Soonie. "Let's go outside and see if we can find something to do."

As she went to the door, Darla clutched her arm. "Where will we go?"

"Oh, I don't know. Perhaps Bright Flower or Tersa has work for us."

"No." Darla shook her head. "I mean, what are you and I going to do when everyone else goes to Fort Sill?"

Soonie froze, her hand hovering over the latch. *Where do I belong?* If Hal or anyone from his group came to the reservation again, they would recognize her. Lone Warrior and Molly too, though Doctor Early would probably find a place to send Molly. The reservation had a school, so they would already have a teacher. She wouldn't be of use. And Darla dreamed about a job in the city. *Chief Quanah is already going to have a large group from the settlement to deal with. He won't want two more people to feed.*

"I'm sure Uncle Isak has already figured it out." Soonie tried to brush away the sadness welling up inside of her. *Everything is changing so fast . . . how can I bear it?*

Soonie and Darla went outside and headed down the path. Tipis were already transformed into tight bundles of hide, their colorful designs hidden away. The long poles that had supported them were too heavy and cumbersome for the wagons, so they would be left behind for the fort soldiers to use as they saw fit.

People bustled around, faces filled with purpose. No tears or anguish were painted on these human canvasses. It was as though all the sorrow and shock of change were left in the school house, replaced with duty and the desire to move on.

Grandmother Eagle came down the hill, carrying rolled blankets and baskets packed with odds and ends. Soonie went over to take some of her burdens and help her load things into a wagon. The oldest adults and youngest children would ride in the wagon beds, along with some of the supplies.

After they arranged everything, Grandmother Eagle turned and patted Soonie's hand. Her wrinkles softened and her eyes filled with peace. "Everything will happen as it should. We cannot change tomorrow, or even the end of today."

How can she be so settled? Here I am, a believer in the true and living God, and my heart quivers like a scared rabbit.

Up on the hill, Bright Flower was busy in the garden by her house. Soonie and Darla hurried to the fence.

"May we help?" asked Soonie.

Bright Flower looked up. Dirt streaked her forehead and settled into worry creases. "Yes. I am taking everything we can eat and burying the plants. Brave Storm wants to make it look like no one lived here for a long time."

Soonie surveyed the neat little garden in dismay. The pumpkins still weren't all ripe, or the squash. Turnips would be half the size they should be. So much time and effort into planting these crops, all for nothing. A small cart sat nearby, already filled with uprooted plants. Her heart sank.

"We will keep what we can." Bright Flower pointed to several baskets containing vegetables in various stages of ripeness. She handed Soonie a hoe. "If you can finish, I need to pack a few more things."

"Of course. We're glad to have something to do," Soonie said.

Darla nodded. "My dad was a farmer, so I know what's what."

"All right." Bright Flower went out of the garden and disappeared inside the tipi.

Soonie began with the pumpkins. She picked every fruit, from the largest, bouncing orange ones to the tiny green ones. Darla came behind her to pull up vines and pile them in the corner.

"Seems like such a waste, doesn't it?" Darla wiped her hands on her apron.

"Every part of this day is filled with waste. If only those men hadn't found Molly and me in the hills!" Soonie caught a wayward pumpkin as it rolled to the ground and placed it back into a basket.

Darla tugged on a strong vine. "Life is full of 'if-nevers.' If my dad hadn't gotten blood poisoning from steppin' on a rake, he would've never kicked the bucket. If he hadn't of died, I'd never have had to become a saloon girl." She squinted over at Soonie. "You must think I'm some kinda sinner, huh?"

"I think you're a brave, amazing woman. And that's the truth," replied Soonie.

"That's kind of you to say." Darla stared down at her button-up shoes, formerly white, but now the color of scalded coffee. "I know who I am, and what I've done. I used to go to church and all. Memorized my Sunday school verses and even sang in the choir. But after dad died, church stuff went out the window." Darla followed Soonie from the pumpkins to the squash.

"You don't have any other family?" Soonie asked.

"Nope." Darla brushed off her hands and tucked a few blond curls back up into her bun. "Lived in a children's home, 'till I came of age. Worked as a maid for a little while, but the misses got jealous of me because of her man's wandering eye and kicked me out. After that, jobs were hard to find." She pressed her hand against her stomach. "You ever been so hungry your belly felt like it was eating itself?"

"No," Soonie said quietly.

"Well, it's not a nice feeling. Like I said, I was desperate. But after what happened with Hal, well, I want to do something different. I don't ever want to feel scared of a man again." Darla bit her lip.

Soonie couldn't imagine this brazen woman ever experiencing fear. But when she remembered Hal's rough grip on her hair, a shiver went down her own spine.

They finished piling the vines and picked up the vegetable baskets. "Let's go ask Bright Flower where we should load these," said Soonie.

"All right," answered Darla. "Hey, Soonie?"

"Yes?"

"Do you think . . . Do you think God still loves me?"

The question was so unexpected, Soonie almost staggered back. "Darla, God loves all of His children, no matter what they do. Nothing can quench that flame, not the darkest of sins. Are you sorry for what you've done?"

Darla looked up. "Yes. I was always sorry. Just didn't feel like I had a choice."

"The Bible says if we ask for forgiveness, He will grant it. There's not a cut-off. No matter how many sins you have in your past, He will forgive you."

"That's a nice thing to know."

Soonie led the way out of the gate. *Should I say more? What else is needed?* A saying from her grandmother trickled into her mind. *A few words, sown in kindness, can grow a great harvest.* For now, she prayed the simple conversation would be enough.

Uncle Isak and Brave Storm were by the fire pit, pouring over drawings in the dirt. Soonie moved closer to hear Uncle Isak's words.

"Gray Fox, Thomas and Bright Flower will ride with the wagons. They have to travel the longer route which will take a few days, but winter is approaching and few go by that path anymore. Two soldiers have agreed to accompany the wagons, with written orders from Captain Wilkerson in case anyone stops them. I'm not sure what story he concocted, but he's very good at such things. He's kept us safe this long."

"And if they meet the posse?" Brave Storm asked.

"Unlikely, but we'll have a scout check the road ahead. If there are any signs of travelers, hopefully they'll have time to move the wagons off the road and hide. Now, Lone Warrior and I will lead the group riding on horseback. We should reach Fort Sill in less than a day, even if we take the forest path. Chief Quanah will find a way to smooth over our return."

Uncle Isak looked up. "Ah. Soonie. I'm glad you are here. There is no need for you to come with us to the reservation. Brother Jenkins will accompany you and Darla to Dallas, and from there you may ride a train home. You have emergency money for a ticket, don't you?"

Soonie nodded numbly. *This will always will be one of the homes of my heart. Oh, why did we have to go foraging on that day? Why can't things stay the same?* Soonie blinked back tears. "Yes, Uncle Isak. I know I can't come along . . . but I wish I could. I'll miss you all so much."

Uncle Isak stood and wrapped her in a hug. "Little One, you have been strong and brave. The love you have shown to these children will warm their hearts forever."

"I . . . I hope so." Soonie pulled out a handkerchief and dabbed at her eyes.

"Please excuse me. I have to check on the horses." Uncle Isak strode off in the direction of the corral.

Soonie scanned the surrounding rocks. "Darla, I'll be back in a moment."

A fall breeze stirred the leaves on the oak by the school house. And he was there, waiting. No paint, no porcupine quills, just himself. Tall, dark and holding her heart somewhere in those strong hands.

Soonie reached up and touched his cheek. "They have arranged for me to go away."

He took her hand and began to trace the lines on her palm. "What will you do, Soo-nie? Go back to your home and become white again?"

She lifted her chin. "I don't want to go. My heart is burning within me. What will you do?"

Lone Warrior sighed. "Soo-nie, I won't live on the reservation. I will go to Fort Sill with the group, to make sure they are safe. Then I will continue on. I believe freedom waits for me in the northern plains, where my forefathers lived."

"North?" The word caught in her throat. "But that's so, so far away."

"Come with me." His tone was calm, but his eyes were intense and pleading. "Come with me, and we will create our own legacy."

Soonie squeezed her eyes shut. *Lord, what should I do? I would miss my family terribly. And they would be so upset if I chose such a dangerous path.* She opened her eyes again.

His face fell.

A sigh bubbled up from her innermost being. "I can't. You know I can't." *Grandma would be sick with grief.*

Lone Warrior held her hand to his heart. It pulsed against her fingers through the rough fabric of his woven shirt. "Do you feel that? It has never beat like this for another. And when you go, it may burst inside of me."

She bowed her head and slowly pulled her hand back. "I'm so sorry."

"I will try to understand." Throwing his shoulders back, he strode off towards the wagons.

Salty drops burned the corners of Soonie's eyes. She pushed into the school room to find Molly packing the few books and papers, most of which belonged to her.

"It's a good thing we don't have much in here," Molly said, tying a stack of books with twine. "Any more and we'd have to leave them behind." She placed the books on top of a small package wrapped in brown paper.

"What is that? I've never seen it before." Soonie picked up the package. "Why, it has my name on it."

She peeled back the top wrapping. "Oh, no."

Molly looked over. "What is it? Captain Wilkerson brought it in when he came earlier."

"The slates," Soonie said in a dull tone.

"Oh, Soonie, I'm so sorry. But they won't take up much room. We will give them to the reservation's school."

Soonie's shoulders slumped. "I'll never get to teach with them, or see the children write on real slates. Molly, why was I called here? I feel like I accomplished so little."

Molly patted her shoulder. "How can you think that way? The children have learned so much already." She paused for a moment, staring at her stack of books. "Sometimes, when I wonder why God has led me down a path, I have to look beyond what I am doing for other people . . . and consider what He is changing inside of me."

Soonie nodded. "You are right, Molly. God has taught me so much since I came. But I still don't want to leave."

"I have lived on the reservation, and I know I'll be all right there," Molly said. "But you would beat your wings to pieces in that place, like a trapped butterfly. You and Lone Warrior are the same."

Soonie could no longer hold back the tears, and they trickled down her cheeks.

Molly gasped. "You do love him! I thought as much. Did he ask you . . .?"

"He asked. I said no." Soonie picked up the package of slates and turned her face away so she wouldn't dot the brown paper with her tears.

When Soonie stepped outside the schoolhouse, Laura was waiting for her. The little girl held out a beaded bracelet. "This is for you, Miss Su."

Soonie ran her fingers over the intricate beadwork. "How beautiful! Did you make this?"

The young girl nodded, her black braids bouncing. "Yes, with the clays. So you wouldn't forget me." She reached up for a hug. "I love you."

"Oh, Laura, I love you too. I could never forget you. Keep studying. Follow after what you want in life, no matter what stands in your way."

Bright Flower came and took Laura's hand. "Come. It's time to get in the wagon." She smiled at Soonie. "Go with God."

Hershel and Felix carried Timothy out of Brave Storm's tipi on a makeshift stretcher.

Timothy waved to her as they passed. "Goodbye, Miss Su!"

Tersa came up and patted Soonie's hand. "The journey will be hard for him, but he is a strong boy. He'll be fine."

For the next hour, goodbyes came in thick flurries. Soonie's face ached from holding back tears. More small gifts were pressed into her hands, and prayers were offered for her journey.

"I want to hold on to everything, every person is so precious," Soonie said to Darla. "But soon they will all ride away from me. There's nothing I can do."

Soonie went back up to the house to fetch her carpet bag.

Molly stood in the middle of the empty room. With the colorful blankets and cheerful glow of the stove gone, the house looked a broken-down shack. It was hard to believe anyone had lived there for a very long time.

"I wanted to give you something." Soonie pressed the silver comb into Molly's hands.

Molly's face lit up. "Thank you. And this is for you."

The cloth she handed Soonie was folded tightly, but Soonie knew it was the painting of their mothers. "Oh, Molly. Someday I'll find a way to come see you. Maybe when you are a famous doctor."

Molly pressed her fingers against her cheeks, and her eyes grew misty. "Someday."

20

The Path Unexpected

Soonie's two gold pieces rested in a pouch around her neck. The money would be enough to get her home, but she worried for Stone Brother. Even if she found a train to transport him, how would he fare on such a journey?

"I can't bear to part with you, not after leaving everyone else," she murmured, patting his quivering neck. "We'll figure something out."

Darla rode beside her, wearing Soonie's one other town dress that wasn't ruined. The former saloon girl had stayed quiet since the beginning of the journey. Her blue eyes held a far-away look.

Soonie had no worries for Darla. She'd been through some tough times, but now she had a chance to leave her past behind and find a decent job.

Lieutenant Ford and another soldier from the fort had been sent by Captain Wilkerson to make sure their little party reached the city safely. They rode a ways ahead with Brother Jenkins. The three men talked, loud laughter punctuating their conversation.

Do they not care about all those people having to return to what is basically a prison? Soonie fought a desire to throw herself at them, to scream out they should be feeling more, caring more. *But I should be thankful,* she reminded herself. *They didn't have to help us reach Dallas.*

The end had come so quickly. Brave Storm had given a handshake, and hugs came from all her students. Uncle Isak, Molly and Grandmother Eagle mixed their tears with hers. But no matter how many times she searched over the faces, she hadn't seen Lone Warrior.

It was probably a good thing. I might have gone into hysterics if I'd tried to say goodbye.

Lieutenant Ford slowed his horse so Soonie could catch up with him. "I've heard tales of dance halls in Dallas. Some stay open all night long." He smoothed the sparse blond hairs forming a new mustache. "No one says you have to jump on the train the minute we get to town. You want to go?"

Soonie blinked. "Go where?"

Darla giggled. "Mercy sakes, girl, he's asking if you want to go dancing."

"You don't think I can dance?" A hint of pink crept up the lieutenant's neck and settled on his ears. "This fellow knows how to take a girl for a turn or two."

"I'm sure you do," Soonie held back a smile. "But once we find a train, I want to board as soon as possible, to avoid any trouble."

"What about you?" Lieutenant Ford turned to Darla. "You're a purty girl. I never found out where you came from. You ever been to a fancy dance hall?"

Darla shot a glance at Soonie. They hadn't told anyone but Molly of her recent profession. "Can't say that I have, Lieutenant Ford. But I can't say that I haven't, either!"

Lieutenant Ford's eyes narrowed, and he tugged his ear. "All right then." He shrugged and urged his horse forward to fall in step with Brother Jenkins and the other soldier.

Soonie glanced over at Darla, who was biting her lip. "What's the matter?"

Darla gave a short laugh. "I'm just wondering what's to become of me. For the last five years I've only known one way to survive, and that's to coax money from weak-hearted men. I don't know how to be respectable."

"I wish you could come home with me, but I don't have any way to get you the extra train fare." Soonie twisted the ends of Stone Brother's reins.

"No, I wouldn't go anyhow. I've had enough of small town life. Everyone knowing the other person's business, and people choosing one man to lead and then going along with whatever he says whether it's right or wrong. I'm going to the city. I can get swallowed up in it, and become a tiny speck no one will pay attention to."

Soonie had her doubts the beautiful girl could lose herself in the city that easily, but she gave what she hoped was a reassuring smile. "I'll be praying for you, every day. And you must write and tell me of all your adventures. Just address it to Bastrop. The post office knows where to find me."

They stopped for a mid-afternoon rest under a gathering of trees. The men talked about hunting and horses, and Darla joined in with silly questions Soonie had a feeling she already knew the answers to.

A small stream gurgled below a rocky bank nearby. Soonie wandered over to listen to the water's music. As the sun dipped lower and the air grew colder, she rubbed her hands together and thought of home. The pumpkin harvest would be coming in, and pecans. Grandpa and Grandma would be thrilled to have her back for Christmas. Zillia's baby would arrive in a few months, and she'd get to hold the child in her arms all fresh and new, before it was old enough to start sassing. And she couldn't wait to see Henry and Will. They'd probably grown a few inches since she'd left.

But Lone Warrior . . .

God, how can I go on? What if I never see him again? She brushed her cheek with her fingers, trying to recall his touch.

Hooves clattered on stone, coming fast around the bend. Breathing hard, Lone Warrior swung down from his horse.

"Soon-ie. Soon-ie."

He is here. Her knees shook.

Lone Warrior's shirt was soaked in sweat, and his eyes held something she had never seen in their depths. *Fear?*

Brother Jenkins leapt to his feet. "What's going on?"

"The posse's heading this way. Hal and that sheriff, and a large group of men."

"The wagons?" Soonie breathed.

"All safe. They didn't get close to the settlement. Maybe those ghost stories are still working. But they're coming right down this road."

Soonie's eyes widened. *He's been with us the whole time. Watching out for me.* "What should we do?"

"Be another few hours before we reach Dallas."
Brother Jenkin's chin trembled.

Lieutenant Ford patted the hilt of his Colt pistol.
"Don't you worry none, Ma'am. We pledged to keep you
safe, and we will do what's needed."

Stone Brother tossed his head and whinnied, loud and
long.

"Let's ride," Soonie said.

Lieutenant Ford frowned. "Lone Warrior, how far
away is the group?"

"About an hour."

Brother Jenkins scanned their faces. "We have time.
We can outrun them."

The other soldier pulled out a pistol. "I'm no
coward."

"Me neither." Darla pulled an impossibly small pistol
from somewhere in the depth of her shawl.

Lone Warrior shook his head. "You would only be
putting yourself at risk. You are wasting time. We all
must ride."

Soonie stepped closer. "I can't stay with them, can
I?"

Lone Warrior stared down at her. "No, Soon-ie."

"Then I have no choice," she said firmly.

A smile played around Lone Warrior's lips, and he
nodded.

Soonie turned to Darla. "Take care of yourself, dear."
She pulled out one of her gold pieces and pressed it into
the girl's hands. "If things don't work out in Dallas, go to
Bastrop and find my family, the Eckharts. They will help
you."

"Don't you think Hal might recognize Darla?"
Brother Jenkins asked.

Darla pulled out the black mantilla from her saddle pack and hung it over her face. She loosened Jimmie's reins from the bush. "Come on, boys; let's see what these horses are made of. Soonie, you've done so much for me. Don't worry about me none. God brought me this far, He'll lead us both to better places."

Brother Jenkins nodded to the soldiers. "Four of us can move faster than two dozen. If Soonie isn't here they will have no reason to bother us even if they do catch up." He nodded to Lone Warrior. "Take care of her."

Lone Warrior grabbed Soonie's hand and they rushed to mount their horses.

"Time to run," Soonie whispered into Stone Brother's ear.

He bolted after Cactus Pear.

Lone Warrior led them to a tricky path through the rocks. She strained to hear any sounds that might suggest conflict behind them, but after the initial thundering of hooves and the normal sounds of bird and wind, all was silent.

For over an hour, they concentrated on riding, neither one of them saying a word. Soonie's heart raced, partially from excitement, and partially in panic. *What have I done? What will we do?*

Lone Warrior was so focused on the path she didn't barrage him with questions, but he suddenly turned as though she had spoken. "Soo-nie, don't worry. After a time we will stop and talk."

She tipped her head to the side. *How does he always know what I'm thinking?*

The path veered north, in the direction of the wild Oklahoma territory. The sun had dipped low behind the clouds by the time they stopped in a wooded area.

Lone Warrior slid off Cactus Pear. He tied the mare to a tree and held out a hand to help Soonie down.

Warmth crept over her face. "Oh my goodness," she murmured.

He frowned. 'What's wrong?"

"Besides worrying about what happened to Darla and the rest of my friends? Or knowing that we have to camp out here tonight, alone? What would my grandparents think? If I even see them again." She slid down from the saddle and buried her face in her hands.

Lone Warrior put his arm around her shoulder. "I know. I'm sorry."

She tilted back and stared into his deep brown eyes. "But you're here, and I thought I'd lost you. But I didn't."

A wide smile covered his impossibly handsome face. "No, you didn't." He touched her chin. "Soo-nie, the trail ahead is one for warriors. We will face danger, and hard times. But I promise to be worthy . . . of your choice."

"You already are," Soonie whispered.

Sparks of happiness danced in his eyes.

Soonie pulled his hand to her cheek and closed her eyes. She would follow this man as the day followed the sun. One day, they would settle somewhere over the hills, in a land where they could be free.

Epilogue

"Hush little baby,
Don't say a word,
Mama's gonna buy you
A mocking bird."

Zillia patted the tiny back, which rose and fell in a peace only slumber could bring. "There we are, little Marjorie Susannah," she whispered.

"Zilly! Zilly!"

The voice was loud and shrill, coming across the farmyard. Zillia stood and tucked the blanket over the sweet, sleeping face. She placed the baby in the cradle and stepped through the door, out to the porch.

"Zilly!" The boy ran through the gate and up the steps. His blond curls stood on end. "Zilly, the postman gave me a letter for you. Guess who it's from?"

Zillia's hand crept over her mouth. "Oh, Orrie, could it be?"

Orrie nodded, his cheeks ruddy from the run. "Yep, it's from Soonie. Open it, Zillie."

Her hands shook as she tore open the flap and opened the precious piece of paper.

March 30th, 1891
Dear Zillia,

I hope you have heard from Brother Jenkins or Darla by now and have learned about the choice I had to make, and why I had to make it. It was a hard thing to do, but Zillia, I promise it was the only way.

By the time you read this, I will be a married woman. Lone Warrior asked me for my hand, and I gave it gladly. We found a tiny mission in the Oklahoma Territory and were married there.

I hope someday, we will have the freedom to come back to Texas and travel in safety. I long to see you all again and wade in my cool Colorado River. Give my love to all, and kiss that sweet baby . . . girl? Or boy? Until then, know I am happy, and being cared for by the love of my life.

Love,
Soonie

A few tears dripped on the words, causing the ink to smear. Zillia wiped them away and pressed the letter to her heart.

God, please care for my friend. And if it's possible, please let me somehow see her again.

About the Author

Angela Castillo has lived in Bastrop, Texas, home of the River Girl, almost her entire life. She studied Practical Theology at Christ for the Nations in Dallas. She lives in Bastrop with her husband and four children. Angela has written multiple stories and books, including the *Westward Wanderers* Oregon Trail series, and the *Toby the Trilby* series for kids. To find out more about her writing, go to http://angelacastillowrites.weebly.com

Excerpt From

The River Girl's Song

Texas Women of Spirit
Book 1, Available on Amazon in paperback and Kindle.

http://www.amazon.com/The-River-Girls-Song-Spirit-ebook/dp/B00X32KBL0/ref=pd_rhf_gw_p_img_1?ie=UTF8&refRID=18DCQ0M4FSR2VYKTRJ15

1

Scarlet Sunset

"We need to sharpen these knives again." Zillia examined her potato in the light from the window. Peeling took so long with a dull blade, and Mama had been extra fond of mash this month.

Mama poured cream up to the churn's fill line and slid the top over the dasher. "Yes, so many things to do! And we'll be even busier in a few weeks." She began to churn the butter, her arms stretched out to avoid her swollen belly. "Don't fret. Everything will settle into place."

"Tell that to Jeb when he comes in, hollering for his dinner," muttered Zillia. The potato turned into tiny bits beneath her knife.

"Don't be disrespectful." Though Mama spoke sharply, her mouth quirked up into a smile. She leaned over to examine Zillia's work. "Watch your fingers."

"Sorry, I wasn't paying attention." Zillia scooped the potato bits into the kettle and pulled another one out of the bag. Her long, slender fingers already bore several scars reaped by impatience.

"Ooh, someone's kicking pretty hard today." Mama rubbed her stomach.

Zillia looked away. When Papa was alive, she would have given anything for a little brother or sister. In the good times, the farm had prospered and she chose new shoes from a catalogue every year. Ice was delivered in the summer and firewood came in two loads at the beginning of winter. Back then, Mama could have hired a maid to help out when the little one came.

She and Mama spent most of their time working together, and they discussed everything. But she didn't dare talk about those days. Mama always cried.

"I might need you to finish this." Mama stopped for a moment and wiped her face with her muslin apron. "I'm feeling a little dizzy."

"Why don't you sit down and I'll make you some tea?" Zillia put down her knife and went to wash her hands in the basin.

Water, streaked with red, gushed from beneath Mama's petticoats. She gasped, stepped back and stared at the growing puddle on the floor. "Oh dear. I'm guessing it's time."

"Are you sure? Dr. Madison said you had weeks to go." Zillia had helped with plenty of births on the farm, but only for animals. From what she'd gathered, human babies brought far more fuss and trouble. She shook the water off her hands and went to her mother's side.

Mama sagged against Zillia's shoulder, almost throwing her off balance. She moaned and trembled. The wide eyes staring into Zillia's did not seem like they could belong to the prim, calm woman who wore a lace collar at all times, even while milking the goats.

Zillia steadied herself with one hand on the kitchen table. "We need to get you to a comfortable place. Does it hurt terribly?"

Mama's face relaxed and she stood a little straighter. "Sixteen years have passed since I went through this with you, but I remember." She wiped her eyes. "We have a while to go, don't be frightened. Just go tell your stepfather to fetch the doctor."

Zillia frowned, the way she always did when anyone referred to the man her mother married as her stepfather. Jeb had not been her choice, and was no kin to her. "Let me help you into bed first."

They moved in slow, shaky steps through the kitchen and into Mama's bedroom. Zillia hoped Mama couldn't feel her frenzied heartbeat. *I have no right to be afraid; it's not me who has to bring an entire baby into this world.*

Red stains crept up the calico hem of Mama's skirts as they dragged on the floor.

A sourness rose in the back of Zillia's throat. *This can't be right.* "Is it supposed to be such a mess?"

"Oh yes." Mama gave a weak chuckle. "And much more to come. Wait until you meet the new little one. It's always worth the trouble."

Mama grasped her arm when they reached the large bed, covered in a cheery blue and white quilt. "Before you go, help me get this dress off. Please?"

Zillia's hands shook so much she could hardly unfasten the buttons. It seemed like hours before she was able to get all forty undone, from Mama's lower back to the nape of her neck. She peeled the dress off the quivering shoulders, undoing the stays and laces until only the thin lace slip was left.

Another spasm ran through Mama's body. She hunched over and took several deep breaths. After a moment, she collected herself and stumbled out of the pile of clothing.

When Zillia gathered the dress to the side, she found a larger pool of blood under the cloth. Thin streams ran across the wood to meet the sunlight waning through the window panes. "There's so much blood, Mama, how can we make it stop?"

"Nothing can stop a baby coming. We just have to do the best we can and pray God will see us through." "I know, Mama, but can't you see... I don't know what to do." Zillia rubbed her temples and stepped back.

Mama's mouth was drawn and she stared past Zillia, like she wasn't there.

Mama won't want the bed ruined. Zillia pulled the quilt off the feather tick and set it aside. A stack of cloths were stored beneath the wash basin in preparation for this day. She spread them out over the mattress and helped her mother roll onto the bed.

Thin blue veins stood out on Mama's forehead. She squeezed her eyes shut. "Go out and find Jeb, like I told you. Then get some water boiling and come back in here as fast as you can."

Zillia grabbed her sunbonnet and headed out the door. "God, please, please let him be close. And please make him listen to me," she said aloud, like she usually prayed.

Parts of her doubted the Almighty God cared to read her thoughts, so she'd speak prayers when no one else could hear. At times she worried some busybody would find out and be scandalized by her lack of faith, but unless they could read thoughts, how would they know?

None of the urgency and fear enclosed in the house had seeped into the outside world. Serene pine trees, like teeth on a broken comb, lined the bluff leading to the Colorado River. Before her, stalks littered the freshly harvested cornfield, stretching into the distance. Chickens scattered as she rushed across the sun-baked earth, and goats bounded to the fence, sharp eyes watching for treats.

"Let Jeb be close!" she prayed again, clutching her sunbonnet strings in both fists. She hurried to the barn. Her mother's husband had spent the last few days repairing the goat fence, since the little rascals always found ways to escape. But he'd wanted to check over the back field today.

Sounds of iron striking wood came from inside. She released the breath she'd been holding and stepped into the gloomy barn.

Jeb's back was towards her, his shirt soaked through. Late summer afternoon. A terrible time for chores in Texas, and the worst time to be swollen with child, Mama said.

"Jeb, Mama says it's time. Please go get the doctor."

"Wha-at?" Jeb snarled. He always snarled when her mother wasn't around. He swung the axe hard into a log so it bit deep and stuck. The man turned and wiped the sweat from his thin, red face. Brown snakes of hair hung down to his shoulders in unkempt strands. "I got a whole day of work left and here it is, almost sunset. I don't have time to ride into town for that woman's fits and vapors. She ain't due yet."

Zillia fought for a reply. She couldn't go for the doctor herself; she'd never leave Mama alone.

Jeb reached for the axe.

"There's blood all over the floor. She says it's time, so it's time." Zillia tried to speak with authority, like Mama when she wanted to get a point across. "You need to go Jeb. Get going now."

When it came to farm work, Jeb moved like molasses. But the slap came so fast Zillia had no time to duck or defend herself. She fell to the ground and held her face. Skin burned under her fingers. "Please, Jeb, please go for help!" she pleaded. Though he'd threatened her before, he'd never struck her.

"Shut up!" Jeb growled. "I'll go where and when I wish. No girl's gonna tell me what to do." He moved away, and she heard the horse nicker as he entered the stable.

Wooden walls swirled around Zillia's head. The anger and fear that coursed through her system overcame the pain and she pushed herself up and stood just in time to see Jeb riding down the road in the direction of the farm belonging to their closest neighbors, the Eckhart family.

They can get here faster than the doctor. First common sense thing the man's done all day. "Please God," she prayed again. "Please let Grandma Louise and Soonie be home."

###

Blood, scarlet like the garnets on Mama's first wedding ring, seemed to cover everything. The wooden floor slats. Linen sheets, brought in a trunk when their family came from Virginia. Zillia's fingers, all white and stained with the same sticky blood, holding Mama's as though they belonged to one hand.

The stench filled the room, sending invisible alarms to her brain. Throughout the birth, they had played in her head. *This can't be right. This can't be right.*\

The little mite had given them quite a tug of war, every bit as difficult as the goats when they twinned. Finally he'd come, covered in slippery blood that also gushed around him.

Over in a cradle given to them by a woman from church, the baby waved tiny fists in the air. His lips opened and his entire face became his mouth, in a mighty scream for one so small. Zillia had cleared his mouth and nose to make sure he could breath, wrapped him in a blanket, and gone back to her mother's side.

Mama's breaths came in ragged gasps. Her eyelids where closed but her eyes moved under the lids, as though she had the fever. Zillia pressed her mother's hand up to her own forehead, mindless of the smear of red it would leave behind.

The burned sun shrank behind the line of trees. No fire or lantern had been lit to stave off the darkness, but Zillia was too weary to care. Her spirits sank as her grasp on Mama's hand tightened.

At some point Mama's screams had turned into little moans and sobs, and mutterings Zillia couldn't understand. How long had it been since they'd spoken? The only clock in the house was on the kitchen mantle, but by the light Zillia figured an hour or more had passed since Jeb left. When the bloody tide had ebbed at last, Zillia wasn't sure if the danger was over, or if her mother simply didn't have more to bleed.

A knock came at the door. The sound she had waited and prayed for, what seemed like all her life. "Please come in." The words came in hoarse sections, as though she had to remind herself how to speak.

The door squeaked open and cool evening air blew through the room, a blessed tinge of relief from the stifling heat.

"Zillia, are you in here?" A tall, tan girl stepped into the room, carrying a lantern. Her golden-brown eyes darted from the mess, to the bed, to the baby in the cradle. "Oh, Zillia, Jeb met Grandma and me in town and told us to come. I thought Mrs. Bowen had weeks to go, yet." She set the light on the bedside table and rushed over to check the baby, her moccasins padding on the wooden floor.

"No doctor, Soonie?" Zillia croaked.

"Doctor Madison was delivering a baby across the river, and something's holding up the ferry. We passed Jeb at the dock, that's when he told us what was going on. The horses couldn't move any faster. I thought Grandma was going to unhitch the mare and ride bareback to get here."

In spite of the situation, Zillia's face cracked into a smile at the thought of tiny, stout Grandma Louise galloping in from town.

An old woman stepped in behind Soonie. Though Grandma Louise wasn't related to Zillia by blood, close friends called her 'grandma' anyway. She set down a bundle of blankets. A wrinkled hand went to her mouth while she surveyed the room, but when she caught Zillia's eye she gave a capable smile. "I gathered everything I could find from around the house and pulled the pot from the fire so we could get this little one cleaned up." She bustled over to the bedside. "Zillia, why don't you go in the kitchen and fill a washtub with warm water?"

Though Zillia heard the words, she didn't move. She might never stir again. For eternity she would stay in this place, willing her mother to keep breathing.

"Come on, girl." Grandma Louise tugged her arm, then stopped when she saw the pile of stained sheets. Her faded blue eyes watered.

Zillia blinked. "Mama, we have help." *Maybe everything will be all right.*

Grandma Louise had attended births for years before a doctor had come to Bastrop. She tried to pull Zillia's hand away from her mother's, but her fingers stuck.

Mama's eyes fluttered. "Zillia, my sweet girl. Where is my baby? Is he all right?"

Soonie gathered the tiny bundle in her arms and brought him over. "He's a pretty one, Mrs. Bowen. Ten fingers and toes, and looks healthy."

A smile tugged at one corner of Mama's pale lips. "He is pink and plump. Couldn't wish for more."

Grandma Louise came and touched Mama's forehead. "We're here now, Marjorie."

Mama's chest rose, and her exhaled breath rattled in her throat. Her eyes never left Zillia's face. "You'll do fine. Just fine. Don't—" She gasped once more, and her eyes closed.

Zillia had to lean forward to catch the words.

"Don't tell Jeb about the trunk."

"Mama?" Zillia grabbed the hand once more, but the strength had already left her mother's fingers. She tugged at her mother's arm, but it dropped back, limp on the quilt.

A tear trickled down Grandma Louise's wrinkled cheek. "Go on to the kitchen, Zillia. The baby should be nearer to the fire with this night air comin' on. Soonie and I will clean up in here."

"I don't want to leave her," Zillia protested. But one glance at her mother's face and the world seemed to collapse around her, like the woodpile when she didn't stack it right.

How could Mama slip away? A few hours ago they'd been laughing while the hens chased a grasshopper through the yard. They'd never spent a night apart and now Mama had left for another world all together. She pulled her hand back and stood to her feet. She blinked, wondering what had caused her to make such a motion.

Soonie held the baby out. His eyes, squinted shut from crying, opened for a moment and she caught a hint of blue. Blue like Mama's.

Zillia took him in her arms. Her half brother was heavier then he looked, and so warm. She tucked the cloth more tightly around him while he squirmed to get free. "I have to give him a bath." Red fingerprints dotted the blanket. "I need to wash my hands."

"Of course you do. Let's go see if the water is heated and we'll get you both cleaned up." Tears brimmed in Soonie's eyes and her lip trembled, but she picked the bundle of cloths that Grandma Louise had gathered and led the way into the kitchen, her smooth, black braid swinging to her waist as she walked.

Zillia cradled the baby in one arm, and her other hand strayed to her tangled mess of hair that had started the day as a tidy bun with ringlets in the front. What would Mama say? She stopped short while Soonie checked the water and searched for a washtub. *Mama will never say anything. Ever again.*

The baby began to wail again, louder this time, and her gulping sobs fell down to meet his.

Zillia sank to the floor, where she and the baby cried together until the bath had been prepared.

As Soonie wrapped the clean baby in a fresh blanket, Jeb burst into the house. He leaned against the door. "The doctor's on his way." His eyes widened when he saw the baby. "That's it, then? Boy or girl?"

"Boy." Soonie rose to her feet. "Jeb, where have you been? I saw you send someone else across on the ferry."

Jeb licked his lips and stared down at the floor. "Well, ah, I got word to the doctor. I felt a little thirsty, thought I'd celebrate. I mean, birthing is women's work, right?"

The bedroom door creaked open, and Grandma Louise stepped into the kitchen. Strands of gray hair had escaped her simple arrangement. Her eyes sparked in a way Zillia had only witnessed a few times, and knew shouldn't be taken lightly.

"Your thirst has cost you dearly, Jeb Bowen." Grandma Louise's Swedish accent grew heavier, as it always did with strong emotion. "While you drank the Devil's brew, your wife bled out her last hours. You could have spared a moment to bid her farewell. After all, she died to bring your child into the world."

Jeb stepped closer to Grandma Louise, and his lips twitched. Zillia knew he fought to hold back the spew of foul words she and her mother had been subjected to many times. Whether from shock or some distant respect for the elderly woman, he managed to keep silent while he pushed past Grandma Louise and into the bedroom.

Zillia stepped in behind him. Somehow, in the last quarter of an hour, Grandma Louise had managed to scrub away the worst of the blood and dispose of the stained sheets and petticoats. The blue quilt was smoothed over her mother's body, almost to her chin. Her hands where folded over her chest, like she always held them in church during prayer.

Tears threatened to spill out, but Zillia held them back. She wouldn't cry in front of Jeb.

The man reached over and touched Mama's cheek, smoothing a golden curl back into place above her forehead. "You was a good woman, Marjorie," he muttered.

"Jeb." Zillia stretched out her hand, but she didn't dare to touch him.

When he turned, his jaws were slack, and his eyes had lost their normal fire. "You stupid girl. Couldn't even save her."

Zillia flinched. A blow would have been better. *Surely the man isn't completely addled? Not even the doctor could have helped Mama.* She shrank back against the wall, and swallowed words dangerous to her own self.

Jeb stared at her for another moment, then bowed his head. "I guess that's that." He turned on his boot and walked out of the room.

Find out more about this book, and Angela Castillo's other writings, at http://angelacastillowrites.weebly.com

Made in the USA
Columbia, SC
18 February 2021